The Spirit of Cochise

The Spirit of Cochise

Elliott Arnold

Hamish Hamilton
London

SBN 241 02333 5

Printed Offset Litho in Great Britain by Cox &
Wyman Ltd, London, Fakenham and Reading

FOR MY FATHER

One

Joe Murdock stood on one side of the store counter facing Old Man Linton. Linton banged his fist on the wood counter. A jar of jelly beans rattled.

"You heard me," Linton shouted. "You don't like the way I run my business you go somewhere else. Now scat!"

Linton said it the way he would shoo a stray dog. Joe remembered back to his childhood and the way Linton always shouted at him and the other Apaches. It reminded him now of the way the noncoms yelled at rookies in the army. When he finally got his own stripes he had tried not to yell. He had to, sometimes, but mostly he tried not to.

Linton yelled some more. There were about twenty other Apaches in the little general store on the San Pedro Reservation in Arizona. Most of them were women. They kept silent and they listened. Some of them were half lost in the darkness of the store. Outside it was a brilliant Arizona day.

Joe listened to Linton and he remembered wondering, back when he was a child, how this store, this same store, could shut off all that light.

Thaddeus Linton closed his mouth. His lips were drawn up like a leather pouch pulled tight by a string. He waited for Joe to make some answer. When Joe wouldn't give him that it made him madder.

He pointed a small, bony finger. "I know all about you, Murdock. I remember you when you were a kid. You made trouble then and looks like you ain't improved none now." Old Man Linton's turkey neck jerked up and down and his finger jabbed the air. "Let me tell you this. Your medals

1

don't buy no goods in my store and them medals don't tell me what to charge." His finger was close enough for Joe to take a bite at it. "I'm telling you once more, get out of my store and let these other people get on with their business here."

Joe didn't answer. The other Apaches were waiting. Their faces dim in the gloom, they knew something was going to happen. They didn't know exactly what it was going to be but they knew it would be something violent and they waited.

Joe breathed in the musty air. It was an old smell to him and he had forgotten it in the years he had been away and now it cut through those years. He remembered when his mother used to bring him into Linton's store. He was Old Man Linton even back then. Joe remembered the jar of jelly beans. He remembered those times his mother used to buy some for him. He remembered that in all the years he had been brought into the store by his mother or his father, from the time when he was a small boy, in all those years Linton had never given away a jelly bean. The memory came back so strong Joe reached out and touched the side of the candy jar.

Linton pulled the jar away. "Get out of here!"

"This is a store," Joe said.

"This is my store."

"People can go into a store."

"Peaceable people. People who want to buy something. Not people who want to make trouble. Now do you get out of here or do I call one of your Apache policemen?"

Joe put both his hands on the counter. The other Apaches felt that whatever was going to happen was getting closer.

"You change your mind, mister?" Linton asked. "You want to buy something?"

"Not at your prices," Joe said.

2

"This is a free country," Linton said. "You just go somewhere else."

The other Apaches listened with Joe. They all knew the same thing. There was a nice country store in Arrowhead, the nearest town outside the San Pedro Reservation, ready and happy to sell anything to any Indian who could manage the forty-five miles. And who had cash to lay on the barrel-head.

Linton hopped up and down like he was standing on red coals. "You heard me! Out!"

Joe expanded his chest a little and the other Indians raised their heads. Joe was not tall but he had the big Apache chest. He was built the way Apaches were built in the old days when they could out-trot a horse hour after hour, when they could live all day on a chew of jerky, when one swallow of water would get them on foot across an Arizona desert that would fry lizards.

His face belonged to those old days too. He was not more than twenty-one and he had one of the true, pure Apache faces. It was a long face and narrow and was made up of planes and angles and was held together by cheekbones that stood out over hollows.

Joe settled down hard in his army shoes and his hands closed on the counter and the army shirt got tight on his chest and back. He didn't need to brace himself for what he was going to do. Tumbling the counter over on Linton was not going to be a hard thing to do.

He leaned against the counter and he thought how the jelly bean jar was going to get broken and he was sorry about that and he got ready to shove. Then he heard a voice behind him.

"Knock it off, Sergeant," the voice said.

Joe didn't move. The muscles in his arms tensed. He didn't turn to see who had spoken to him. It had been a white man's voice. He knew that. Joe kept his hands on the counter and

3

waited for more words from that voice. He had learned in the army that when someone gives an order and means it he only gives it once. Joe dropped his hands from the counter and turned. Just inside the store entrance he saw a white man. The white man was about forty or so. He was spare and he had a flat belly. Joe judged a man by his belly. He had found out in the army that when you needed men to go out on a patrol it was good sense to choose people with no lard. It reflected the mentality of the man and how he respected his body and himself.

Joe waited for the white man to tell him again to knock it off. Then he might tell the white man to go to hell and he might turn back and do what he started to do. The white man didn't give him that opening. They might have stood there a long time. In the end Joe might have still dumped the counter, not only because of Linton but because of the white man as well.

Linton saved it. He started to scream again. For some reason that Joe couldn't figure out it made him feel good. It didn't rile him. He wanted to laugh at the crazy shouting behind his back. It was so funny he twisted around and had another look at Old Man Linton and he saw a little man who didn't top the counter by very much, who had strands of dirty yellow-white hair and a tobacco-stained moustache. Joe wondered why the sutler had never looked funny to him before.

He straightened up. He could almost hear the silence of the other Apaches. He knew they had been expecting something. He put one hand back on the counter. He rocked the counter just a little. Just so the jelly bean jar slid a couple of inches, nothing more. He held the counter tilted toward Linton who had stopped speaking but who kept his mouth open. Then Joe let the counter settle back slowly. He moved the candy jar to exactly where it had stood before.

4

"You're a thief," he said to Linton in a voice that had been honed by all the time he had worn the stripes, by all the time he had moved men around in the Viet Nam jungles. "You ought to be buried up to your neck. You ought to have your face covered with honey. You ought to have ants turned loose on you."

He went out of the store. Even in the darkness he could see the look on the Apache faces, the look brought on by his invocation of an almost forgotten Apache torture.

Two

Outside the sun hit him with a wallop that almost blinded him. He blinked his eyes, wondering whether he had done the right thing. He wondered whether he had not dumped the counter because he had thought better of it or because he had backed down before white authority. He wondered whether the army had given him something or had robbed him of something. He hadn't known exactly what it was going to be when he got back to San Pedro but he knew it was not going to be very good. He had been back less than a week now and he knew it stronger than ever.

After a few moments his eyes went back to work and he looked at the outside of Linton's store. He had seen it as far back as he could remember but he looked at it now as though he had never seen it before. His father had told him once that the building had been put up almost a hundred years ago when the reservation was established. Like all the other official buildings it was made of gray stone. Now it was almost black. All the government buildings were almost black now, the administration buildings, the little houses in which the white Bureau personnel lived, the guest houses, the storage buildings. That was something he couldn't understand. The air here was the purest in the world. He used to dream of this air in the Nam swamps. The air was sweet and clean and dry and it couldn't make anything else black. The air could bleach anything white, given time, yes. But somehow it had made the buildings of the Bureau of Indian Affairs look like they lived in soot.

Joe filled his lungs. He was shaking a little. Maybe it wasn't shaking, not the shaking that meant fear, anyway.

He heard footsteps and turned around. It was the white man who had given him the order in Linton's store. Now in the sunlight in his shirt sleeves the white man didn't seem to have all that authority. Joe wondered again why he had obeyed him. Had it been the army discipline or had he slipped back into his reservation skin that fast?

He looked at the white man warily. Here, on this reservation, on the land Joe's people had lived on and had hunted on and had killed on before there were any white men, he was now in white man's country. On an army post there was officers' country and enlisted men's country. But here there was no Indian country. Not even when you got away from the dirty government buildings, far away, into the Indian woods. They weren't Indian woods any more.

The white man said, "I'm Bill Hunter."

He didn't hold out his hand. Joe liked that. He never understood why white men always had to shake hands. Like it was a secret grip in the white man's fraternity.

"I guess you know me, Mr. Hunter," Joe said.

There was nothing else he could call the white man but it sounded to Joe as though he were calling him Colonel or Major or Sir. He was a little mixed up about that and to straighten himself out he looked at the building again.

"That thieving bastard," he said. He wanted the white man to know that while he had backed down on action inside the store he hadn't backed down on his feelings.

Hunter didn't say anything.

"Do you buy in there?" Joe asked.

"Not very often."

"Do you know what the prices are in there?"

"I think so."

"Double what they are outside. Some things three times as much, maybe. You know what he charges for a pack of cigarettes?"

"Yes."

Joe kept staring at the building. "I remember when I was a kid everybody used to say he was in cahoots with the Agent otherwise he couldn't get away with it."

Hunter remained silent. After a while Joe looked at him. Joe's eyes were dark almost all over, hardly any whites in them at all. In the old days the Apaches used to refer to white men contemptuously as "white-eyes."

"I didn't hear you, Mr. Hunter," Joe said.

"I didn't say."

Joe looked at him closer. "You must be one of them."

"I'm Deputy Agent."

Hunter pushed a pack of cigarettes up out of his shirt pocket. He offered one to Joe. Joe looked at the pack a long time before he accepted.

Some of the Apaches who had been in the store were coming out now. They saw Joe talking to the white man and they went by without saying anything.

"Maybe you can tell me something, Mr. Hunter," Joe said. "Maybe you can tell me why the Tribal Council doesn't do something about Linton."

"When did you get back, Joe?"

"Do you know why the Council sits tight for this?"

"No."

"This is supposed to be our reservation."

Hunter nodded.

Joe looked at the burning end of his cigarette. "In Nam lots of guys rapped about what they called the establishment. I didn't know what they were talking about then. They used to say everybody has an establishment and that all establishments worked together. There were blacks who used to say there even was a black establishment that was closer to the white establishment than it was to its own people. Maybe that's the way it is with the Tribal Council."

8

"I wouldn't know."

"Wouldn't you?"

"Why don't you ask them?"

More women came out. They hurried by.

"You telling me to make trouble with the Council, Mr. Hunter?"

"I'm saying if you have a question about the Council put it to the Council. You have that right."

Joe nodded. "Like Linton said, it's a free country."

Joe felt the inside of himself going away. He had once been told by an officer, an educated officer, that people had to have the enemy on their necks for a long time before they could go away like that. He thought that must be true. He had seen blacks do the same thing and he knew it must be true.

He knew he was standing there with a white man, smoking a white man's cigarette, and that the white man was less than two feet away. But he had shut the white man out and if the white man had walked away he almost wouldn't have known it. He wondered if the white man had that same kind of protection. Like armor, inside.

At that moment he heard someone running. He looked up to see Jennie. She was out of breath and her eyes were frightened. She put her hand on Joe's arm. It lost itself there, a browny-red starfish.

"Joe, what happened?"

Joe shifted uncomfortably. "Nothing."

The protection was gone and he was back again and he felt embarrassed. Didn't she know Apaches didn't act this way in public, especially not in front of white people?

"I heard you were in some trouble with Mr. Linton," Jennie said, her pretty face filled with concern.

"It wasn't anything."

Joe liked Jennie Gates. While he was away he thought of

her as his girl. He wrote to her and she wrote to him. But she should know better than to act this way out in the open.

She shook her head. "I was afraid something like this was going to happen."

She looked up at him as though he was something holy but Joe didn't see that. He was twisting his head this way and that to see whether anybody besides the one white man was watching this.

"Nothing happened, Jennie," Hunter said.

"Because you stopped it, Mr. Hunter," she said. "If you hadn't stopped it there would have been real trouble."

"I didn't stop him. He had second thoughts, was all."

She bit her lips. "Joe, you have to realize you're back here now. Things are different."

"I know," Joe said. He wished she would stop hanging on his arm. But he couldn't make any move that would hurt her feelings.

He knew what she meant. It was funny, he supposed. Most guys felt that getting out of the army was like getting out of jail. With him it was like returning to jail. He supposed it was funny.

"Well, I got to get back to work," Hunter said. He left.

Joe was grateful for that. He would have to explain to Jennie that this kind of thing couldn't happen again. He would have to make her know certain feelings were private.

"Joe, promise me you won't get into trouble," she said.

"Don't you have to get back to work too?" he asked.

She took away her hand. He walked away.

Three

Joe opened his eyes and saw the cracked plaster on the ceiling. For a moment he didn't know where he was. He tensed, as though to spring. Then he remembered, and he relaxed. He would have to get used to sleeping alone in the bedroom he had shared with his brother all his life. Larry was married now and he and his wife and their first child lived in their own place. His sister, Lou, had got herself married before Joe went off to the war and she had a house and kids.

Now there was just himself and his mother and his father and he had the bedroom for himself and Lou's bedroom just stood empty as it had stood empty for years because his mother and father couldn't think of any way to put it to use. It was a guest room, only there never were guests.

Nobody wanted to be a guest on an Indian reservation. There was the official guest house among the other official buildings but the only guests who stayed there were people on business from the Indian Bureau and they left as soon as they could.

Joe sat up and swung his feet around. The suitcase he had brought back was still lying open on the other bed. He had taken out his bathroom things but very little else. He rubbed his chin. He could stand a shave. Somebody once had told him he had a full beard for an Indian. It had irritated him at first and then he had felt proud and then after that he felt ashamed he had felt proud.

He decided against shaving. For what? He had no reason. There was nothing to do. He had had nothing to do since he had returned. He'd go to work on something soon but right now he had nothing to do. He didn't know how to handle idleness. Over in Nam, there had been a lot of that, especially toward the end, but it wasn't the same. You loved idleness because the next day you might not be around. It was always like the last day in the death house.

He stood up and got dressed. He put on old levis and a shirt. The levis still fit him but the shirt was a little tight around the shoulders. He must have put on some heft. Or maybe the shirt had shrunk and he had forgotten about it. He went out of the room.

His mother and father were sitting in the room that served as kitchen and living room. His mother was cutting up left-over meat and potatoes and vegetables for a stew. His father had his bad leg resting on a stool. They had the radio on. When Joe entered the room his father turned down the radio. His parents looked at him questioningly. They didn't ask questions, they looked questions. Joe knew his father wanted to know how it had been over there, about the fighting, what it was like, but he didn't want to talk about it. Not yet. Maybe never, but certainly not yet.

He said good morning to his parents and poured himself some coffee. His father filled a pipe and shifted his bad leg. As far back as Joe could remember his father had that bad leg. He had been thrown from a horse while working as a wrangler on the range with the tribal herd of cattle. The horse had thrown him right into the horns of a steer. Oliver Murdock had been gored the way a bullfighter gets gored. They didn't set his leg very well at the reservation clinic and the bone healed badly and he always limped after that. The leg usually hurt, some times worse than others. The pain was on his father's face, in the thin lines around his mouth and at the outsides of his eyes. Oliver Murdock never spoke about it.

"Are you hungry, Joe?" Florence Murdock asked. She was a small woman with gray hair.

"No, Mom," Joe said.

"You don't eat in the morning anymore," she said. "You used to eat so much in the morning."

"Sit down, Joe," Oliver said. He flicked a wooden match into light with his thumbnail and held the flame over the pipe bowl and hauled in gulps of smoke.

The room filled with the smell of pipe smoke. For a moment it made Joe feel he had never been away at all.

"I heard you had some trouble with Mr. Linton," Oliver said.

Florence Murdock looked up nervously.

"It wasn't much," Joe said, sitting down on a chair at the table.

"Joe," Oliver started.

"Don't tell me things are different," Joe said.

"Joe," his mother said.

"I'm sorry."

"We need Mr. Linton," Oliver said.

"Yes."

"What happened?"

"I guess I just had forgotten what a thief he was."

Oliver Murdock took the pipe out of his mouth. He looked worried. Joe hated to see that look.

"Then you did call him that?" Oliver asked.

"Yes."

"That's what they told me. I hoped it wasn't true."

His father looked frightened now. Oliver rubbed his bad leg. Joe had always been proud that his father had never complained about the pain in his leg. Now he wondered maybe it wasn't because he was a man about that but because he was afraid of the white authorities.

"Did you tell him he ought to be buried and eaten by ants?" Oliver asked.

"Yes." Joe put down the coffee cup.

Oliver broke into a laugh. It was an unexpected sound in

the room. Joe looked at him, startled, and then he grinned. He was ashamed of what he had just been thinking about his father.

"He ought to be, too," Oliver said.

Joe saw his mother open her mouth to say something and then close it. It was a good feeling, Joe thought. It was the way a house should be. Even with his bad leg and his book-keeping job his father was still boss of the house.

"He told me it was a free country," Joe said. He felt easier. He even felt like talking. "He told me if I didn't like the way he ran his store to go somewhere else."

Oliver frowned and looked worried again. "Joe, you know it would be bad if we had to buy goods somewhere else."

"It would be cheaper."

"Arrowhead is far away and the stores there won't give credit."

"They're fools," Joe said.

"How are they fools?"

"They're missing a chance to keep books the way Linton keeps them."

Oliver Murdock looked around to make certain nobody was eavesdropping. Joe hated to see that.

"Nobody has ever proved Mr. Linton cheats on his accounts," Oliver said.

"Has anybody checked? Ever?"

"It wouldn't be proper."

"Do you keep a record? From one end of the year to the next?"

"No."

"Then how do you know? You keep the tally for the work done on the range and you know about those things and even you don't keep accounts with Linton. You charge things and after the cattle sale you pay Linton whatever that thief tells you you owe him. How do you know he isn't charging you more than you bought?"

14

"He has everything written down. We sign each time we buy."

"He can give you any figure he wants, can't he? He just tells you the total amount, doesn't he? He doesn't bother to show you all the markers, does he?"

Oliver had let his pipe go out and he made a ceremony of relighting it. "Mr. Linton has been here for a long time."

Joe slapped his hand on the table. "*Mr.* Linton. *Mr.* Linton."

"Joe," Mrs. Murdock said.

"I'm sorry, Mom," Joe said.

Oliver got his pipe going again and Joe smelled the smoke and he thought about how it was when his brother and sister were around and the house seemed smaller but happier. Now there was nobody else to talk to but his parents. It used to bounce off three and now it just bounced off one.

"Well, Son, how does it feel to be home?" Oliver asked, changing the subject.

"All right," Joe said, thinking it a silly question.

"It will take a little time."

"Yes."

"You haven't told us much how it was outside."

They all called it "outside," Joe thought. After all these years it was still "outside." The way prisoners call it "outside." The reservation wasn't really a prison. Anybody could leave anytime he liked. He had known of some who had tried and who had come back. Even some who had gone to college. It wasn't just the color of the skin, they said, it was the way an Indian thought that made it tough for him outside.

Except in the army. In the army you got shot at the same way no matter what your skin color was and no matter what you thought about things, and when you were shot they patched you up the same way. They gave you the same medals.

15

"What about your medals?" Oliver asked.

"What about them?"

"I want to put them in a frame like a picture. I want to hang them on the wall. I told you that."

Joe nodded.

"When will you have it done?"

"Next time I get to Arrowhead."

Joe stood up. He liked the room with the familiar furniture but it was closing in on him now.

"Be careful," his mother said.

"Talk to the people," his father said. "The people are proud of you."

"It's a lousy, stupid war, Pop," Joe said.

"Maybe it is. But the people are proud of you. Talk to them. It will make them feel good."

"Okay, Pop." He felt sad.

"Apaches were always warriors," Oliver said, shifting his game leg. "They are proud of men who have fought well. Even in bad wars. Talk to them and make them feel good."

Joe nodded.

"Sam Hopkins, the man who lives down the road. He was in the army once. Talk to him."

"Okay, Pop."

"And don't irritate Mr. Linton anymore."

"No, Pop."

"We were always a fighting people. The people will be happy to listen to you."

Joe nodded and went to the door.

"We never surrendered," Oliver Murdock said. "The President of the United States sent an important general out to Arizona to make peace with Cochise."

Joe had heard that story more than once.

"The general came out and asked Cochise to make peace," Oliver said. "He told Cochise the President was pleading for peace. We never surrendered."

16

But afterward we were screwed, Joe thought. He went out the door, looking back at his father's house. It was a pleasant little cottage. He supposed the Apaches were lucky. They lived a little better than Indians on most other reservations. That was because of their beeves.

At that moment he liked the little cottage very much. He even liked the wickiup in back of the house. His parents, like most of the other Apaches, had this little hut in the backyard. It was the kind of hut they used to live in in the old days when they moved around a lot. It could be taken down and put up in minutes. They didn't use it for living in now. They used it for storage, but it meant more than that, Joe knew. When he was a kid some of the white people on the reservation used to laugh at the wickiups. They said it only showed that after all these years the Apaches hadn't really changed. They were still savages. It had made Joe feel ashamed. The Apaches could have built ordinary sheds in their backyards and then the white people wouldn't laugh. It made him think too much about the kind of people he had come from. Then, after he had been in Viet Nam for a little while he had come to understand why they were there.

The wickiups made the Apache people forget a lot of things and remember a lot of other things. The wickiup in his own backyard made his father feel good and helped him to forget the pain in his leg.

Four

He hadn't seen the Agent for a long time now but the Agent hadn't changed. The Agent was part of his childhood, like the darkness in Linton's store and the smell of his father's pipe.

The Agent reminded him of a general he had seen in Viet Nam. He guessed the Agent would have been flattered to hear that.

Townsend Lawton was a very elegant man. He was as handsome as his official government picture. He was just past sixty and he had white hair and a cropped moustache. He did a lot of riding and he liked to wear riding clothes. Sometimes the Agent wore jodhpurs. He even used an English saddle and Joe remembered the Apaches had always stopped to stare at that.

He was not wearing a riding outfit now but he had his riding crop on his desk and every once in a while he fiddled with it. He was trying to outstare Joe. Joe smiled to himself. The Agent knew more about a lot of things than he did but he couldn't match Joe at being silent and staring. That was something Joe was born knowing about.

Lawton, now tapping the riding crop against the palm of his hand, gave up. "I'm sorry that our first meeting since your return is under these circumstances, Joe."

Joe didn't know what the circumstances were. So he said nothing. He was ready to start staring again.

"I thought you might have paid a call on me when you first got back," Agent Lawton said.

Joe wondered why he thought that. Lawton was famous for not liking to have Indians barge into his office.

"How long have you been back?" Lawton asked, shifting to direct questioning.

"Ten days or so."

"Just out of courtesy. Wouldn't you have thought that, Mr. Hunter?" He raised an eyebrow at his Deputy.

"I guess it's all the way you look at it," Hunter said.

The Agent frowned, not entirely satisfied with that answer. Joe looked out the window. It was another clean day. He wondered why he was in the Agent's office.

"I was disappointed, Joe. It isn't often we have a genuine war hero return to the fold."

The Agent was saying it straight, Joe thought. He wondered why it didn't reach him that way.

"Bronze Star, two Purple Hearts, a sergeant's rating. You must be pleased with yourself, Joe." Lawton smiled pleasantly. "But then I suppose we shouldn't be at all surprised. You Apaches have a tradition for being expert at that kind of thing."

Joe looked straight ahead. There was nothing wrong with the words, but they didn't get there good.

"And that particular kind of fighting," Lawton said, still smiling. "In the jungles, sneaking up on the enemy, that's precisely your cup of tea, isn't it, Joe?"

Joe looked out the window.

"I imagine the only type of soldier who could get around more quietly in the jungle than a Viet Cong would have to be an Indian," Lawton said. "Well, enough of that." He got on his feet and began to pace back and forth. "What was the problem in Mr. Linton's store?"

"The prices." Now Joe knew why he was there.

"What about the prices?"

"They're sky-high."

Lawton pursed his lips and nodded soberly. "Is that your opinion, Joe?"

19

"It's no opinion."

Lawton paused and fixed his eyes on Joe. "You were in the service three years, weren't you?"

"Yes." He was not about to "sir" the Agent. Many of the Apaches did but he'd had a bellyful of that.

"While you were in uniform you received the benefits of greatly reduced prices on many things due to the generosity of the taxpayers. Beer, cigarettes. Things like that."

Joe didn't say anything.

"Then it's only normal for you to be surprised, even shocked, at what civilians have to pay for things."

"I'm not talking about prices on a base exchange," Joe said. "I'm talking about prices in ordinary stores outside the reservation. Linton is robbing everybody blind."

"You might think that, Joe," Lawton said.

Joe saw that the Agent had now put on his patient face. A lot of the Apaches felt Lawton talked to them as though they were children, stupid children.

"I'm sure you don't know much about economics, Joe," Lawton said.

"Nothing."

"Then you wouldn't understand how expensive it is to ship things here to the reservation. Mr. Linton has great costs, far beyond the costs of storekeepers on the outside. And he's in business to make a reasonable profit."

"He's robbing everybody blind. And please don't tell me that anybody who doesn't want to deal with Linton can go somewhere else. There used to be a bus running to Arrowhead. What happened to that?"

"It went out of business, Joe. Not enough of you people used it. Regrettable, I admit. But the bus people had to make a reasonable profit too. That's what I mean by economics. It's something you Apaches find hard to understand. But then you're not altogether to blame for that. You've never

20

had to go out and struggle in free competition on the open market. You've been supported by the government for a long time."

Lawton walked around his desk and sat down in his big chair. "What I have to say to you is simply this, Joe. I have not had the opportunity to speak to either Mr. Linton or Mr. Hunter so I don't know the details of what occurred in the store. I intend to find out. But I will tell you now that you are going to have to make a serious adjustment here. You never were a tractable boy, as I remember. There are more than four thousand Indians on my reservation, yet I can still remember what a difficult boy you were. And now of course your war experiences have undoubtedly developed other uncivilized instincts in you. We are all grateful for your war service to our country but it is my duty to remind you that you now are back on the reservation."

The stillness came over Joe again.

"I run an evenhanded reservation here, governed by rules and regulations that have been tested over the years," Lawton went on. "At San Pedro every Indian is treated the same as every other Indian. That includes war heroes. I will point out that I will tolerate no violence. Is there anything you want to say before you go?"

"No," Joe said.

"Then I'll assume that we understand each other and that what happened in Mr. Linton's store was an error in judgment and will not be repeated in any way." The Agent stood up. He smiled brilliantly. "Welcome home, Sergeant Murdock." He walked over to Joe and put his hand on Joe's shoulder. "I know that we are going to get along together splendidly."

Joe walked to the door. Hunter followed.

"Mr. Hunter," Lawton said.

"Yes, sir?"

21

"I have an appointment with Mr. Linton at two-thirty. Will you please report here at three o'clock and give me your version."

Five

Joe walked down the corridor from the Agent's office. The walls were lined with pictures of important people, starting with the President of the United States. He entered a large room where thirty or forty people were working at desks piled up with paper work. He remembered when he went to school on the reservation he had been told by a teacher that San Pedro was large, almost twice the size of Rhode Island.

He saw Jennie Gates working at her desk. She looked up as he passed. He kept walking. He didn't want her to get up and run over to him in front of all the other people.

Jennie Gates. It was a crazy name for an Apache woman. His own name was a crazy name for an Apache man. He remembered one evening in Nam when someone had asked him how come he had a name like Murdock instead of Running Bear or Moon-in-the-Sky. One of them had suggested Sergeant Pain-in-the-Ass. They all had laughed. Joe had made his way by then and they kidded him about anything, and with respect and affection.

Joe had told them what he had been told in school. That when the Apaches first were put on the reservation the authorities, usually army officers, couldn't understand Apache names. They had to fill out their rosters. It was a head count for supplies. So they put down whatever names came to their minds, the names of other officers, soldiers, friends, later on names out of the telephone book. The teacher had told him that they used to do the same thing back East at a place called Ellis Island where Immigration people gave nice, simple American names to foreigners.

Almost everybody on the reservation had a good American name and they were supposed to be proud of that but Joe was not proud. He was confused. The name somehow didn't fit. He would like to have had an Apache name but Murdock had been his family name for quite a few generations now and there was no other name he knew. Whatever the original Apache name had been now was lost for all time.

There was one Apache on the San Pedro land who had an Indian name. That was Nahilzay. Nahilzay was said to be one hundred years old and he probably was older than that. He was the elder statesman of the tribe. He was a permanent member of the Tribal Council. He attended all the meetings, sitting apart from all the other councilmen, a war staff with three eagle feathers in his hands. His name was that of one of the great Cochise's best war lieutenants. It was said this Nahilzay was given that famous name because he was brave. He was a spirit from the past and his mind was sharp and clear and he was listened to.

Joe would like to talk to Nahilzay. He knew he never would dare.

As he stepped outside the dark stone building, he felt lighter, easier, less tense. It was one of those Arizona days he had thought about when he was away. He could almost count the leaves on trees half a mile away. The sky was scrubbed clean blue and the air had a sparkle. Joe was grateful his ancestors had been wise enough to settle in Arizona.

He saw the white Deputy, Hunter, step out of the building. This time Joe offered him a cigarette.

"The question is, Mr. Hunter, do I look like a snake?" Joe said after a moment.

Hunter shook his head soberly. "No, Joe, I can't say you do."

"A rattler. Something that creeps through the grass and can catch even a VC by surprise."

"Maybe it was his way of paying a compliment."

24

Joe looked at Hunter solemnly. He held up his hand. "Let not the white man speak with a forked tongue."

"All right. I read you." Hunter smiled.

"I know what side you're on, Mr. Hunter. You have to be on the side the bread comes from. We don't have to bull each other, do we, Mr. Hunter?"

"No."

"We had a captain like Lawton once. He looked like a movie actor too. He wasn't a bad officer. He was smart and he had guts. Only he didn't exactly feature people whose skin was darker than his and his was pretty light."

"Then it wasn't all that easy out there."

"It's never easy, Mr. Hunter. It's never easy being different."

"You're sure as hell not different here. If there's anybody different it's us."

Joe considered that. "In the army it was something else. You were different, sure. Even if you were good at your job, you were different. I was good. They liked me, maybe. You made friends and maybe that was because they liked you or maybe it was because fighting, that kind of fighting, was in your bones. It was nothing they taught me. The Agent was right about that. But still you were different. There weren't too many red Indians. You stood out. The blacks had each other, a hell of a lot of each other. Not us." Joe looked at his cigarette. "They used to make jokes. They used to say when I killed someone that I mustn't scalp them. They used to say that was against regulations. They even made up a fake regulation against scalping once. At first I tried to answer them. I tried to explain Apaches never scalped. That Apaches were the ones who were scalped by the white bounty hunters working for the Mexican authorities. They wouldn't buy that. Too many movies. So for a long time I had to listen to a lot of smartass grunts tell me I couldn't scalp the enemy. And each one thinking he was the first one to think that up. Then after a while it died off. Maybe it was because I started getting stripes."

"And bullets," Hunter said.

"But there was a difference. One difference. If they thought I was an oddball that was their privilege and once or twice in the beginning I had to beat up on someone. But it was a personal thing. The difference was that as far as army rules and regs were concerned I was no different from any other guy. There were no special rules for soldiers who happened to be Chiricahua Apaches."

"There was a Cheyenne in my company," Hunter said.

Joe looked up. "Where was that?"

"Korea."

Joe looked closely at Hunter. Then his mouth tightened as Thaddeus Linton ran by on his way to keep his appointment with the Agent. Linton glared at Joe as he passed.

"I never knew a Cheyenne," Joe said. He felt himself withdrawing inside. He knew when Linton was finished with Lawton it would be this white man's turn.

"His name was Redbow. Bob Redbow. I used to listen to him," Hunter said. "I guess that's why I got into this business when I got out."

"Does he know that?" Joe was still watching Linton as the old man scurried into the administration building.

"He was killed. He was killed saving my life, among others."

Joe turned his eyes on Hunter. "How was that?"

"It was on one of those Korean hills, the ones they gave numbers to. We'd been bushwhacked one night and we were trying to get away and he was killed. He stayed back, covering for the rest of us."

"Maybe he was just trying to get himself an enemy scalp," Joe said and walked off.

26

Six

During the next week or so Joe worked around the house, doing things his father hadn't been able to do because of the bad leg. He put new shingles on the roof and painted the kitchen and fixed the corral in the back where they kept goats. His brother Larry used to keep things fixed up but now Larry had his own place to worry about.

Working around the house Joe got to know his mother and father a little better. He had known them pretty well, he thought, when he was a kid, but he had to get to know them all over again as a man, with all the things he had learned the three years he was away.

He visited Larry and his sister, Lou, a couple of times. He was glad to see them and their kids but he didn't feel very close to them anymore.

One day he was fixing the flue in the kitchen stove and he said to his father, "How does anybody ever know whether it's the stove smoking up the room or your pipe?"

Oliver Murdock laughed. It was good to have his youngest child back home. Not as good as the old days when all the children were there, but good. Also he was relieved that Joe seemed to be content working at home doing chores. After what happened at the sutler's store he hadn't known which way his son was going to go.

Joe knew he would have to start working soon, but he wasn't worried about money at the moment. He had his army money saved up. His family was not in great need of it. Although Oliver Murdock couldn't ride the herd anymore he kept tally on the books for those who did tend the beeves.

The hours the men worked were recorded and that's how their pay was determined after the cattle sale.

The time came when Joe began to run out of things like toothpaste and shaving cream and cigarettes. His old army shirts were wearing out and for some reason he didn't want all of them to go. He wanted to keep one. He didn't know why.

He needed things but he could not bring himself to go to the sutler's store. He thought about asking his father to buy the necessities but he decided he could not do that. Even if Linton didn't know the goods were for him, he couldn't do it. There was something inside that wouldn't let him.

He solved one problem by quitting cigarettes. Still, as days passed, and he worked hard around the house, he knew he had to get himself some clothes. Even his army shoes weren't going to last forever.

One night Mel Moore came over to the house to pay his father a visit. Mel Moore was a tribal judge and his father's good friend.

Moore had fought in the South Pacific in World War II. He and another Chiricahua Apache were used in New Guinea to send messages back and forth on the radio. They sent the messages in Apache. The Japanese never broke that code. After the war Cpl. Moore went to college on the GI bill. He learned a lot and he played football.

He was always a big man and after he returned to San Pedro he began to put on weight. He was a mighty eater and a mighty drinker of tiswin, the Apache beer that was illegal but which was brewed by old women in backyards.

Mel Moore got to be enormous. It was said his levis hung so low on his hips they were in danger of falling down and his belly hung over them like a balloon. He was given a long Apache nickname, which meant The-Man-Who-Is-Pregnant.

That made Mel Moore ashamed and he took off a hundred

28

pounds and became known among his cronies as The-Man-Who-Had-a-Baby. But the effort of dieting had a strong effect on him and he became a serious and industrious man who worried about his people. He became a tribal judge and was one of the best.

Joe didn't mind talking about the war with Judge Moore. He had been in one himself. On this night while he was smoking a cigar and sitting comfortably in the best chair in the room, he asked Joe about drugs in Viet Nam.

"I hear they use a lot of that stuff out there," the Judge said.

"I think so," Joe said.

"How about you?"

"I didn't need it."

"Why do the others need it?"

"I don't know. Maybe because it's a bad war and it goes nowhere."

"All wars are bad wars unless you are defending your own land."

Joe's mother and father sat to one side. They were proud that the Judge was speaking to Joe man to man.

After a while, Joe said, "It was better for me than for some of the others. I was used to living in the open and to things being rough. I never needed any of that stuff floating around. Some of the others, especially the ones from cities, the blacks and the whites, they're lost there in Nam. They don't know why they're there and they don't know what they're dying for. Nobody ever told them so they'd know. Maybe you can't blame them for trying to buy themselves dreams."

"How do they do their jobs?" Judge Moore asked.

"I don't know. Some of my men smoked pot. I couldn't stop that. None of them used hard stuff, far as I knew. I'd have busted any man for that."

Oliver Murdock took his pipe out of his mouth and cleared

his throat. This was the happiest evening since Joe had come back. "We hear bad things from over there."

"There are bad things," Joe said.

"Mylai. What about that place?" Oliver asked.

"As far as I know it happened," Joe said.

"Were you there?" Moore asked.

"No. I saw things like that at other places."

"It's hard to believe," Oliver Murdock said.

"Why is it hard to believe?" the Judge asked. "American Indians have had hundreds of Mylais. We Apaches alone can count a dozen or more. It is in the classic tradition of the American army to shoot up villages with women and children and old people. Custer was famous for that. And what is different between Mylai and the Camp Grant Massacre?"

Joe said, "I would like to know more about those things."

"It was the reason Cochise fought the army so long. He didn't trust any one of them. He had learned of too many times when the cavalry had itself a little Mylai," Moore said.

"Where can I find out more about those things?" Joe asked.

"Read about them," the Judge said. "One thing about the American whites, when they do something bad they usually expose it. It may take a little time but eventually they expose it. It's all in books, Joe. Read about it. A lot of it has been put down and some of it has even been put down true. Read about it. And talk to me. I know about Indian history."

Judge Moore left about ten. As he was going out the door, he said to Joe, "It must be rough being stuck here on the reservation after being on the outside so long. And you must need things and I guess you don't want to do business with Linton."

Joe looked at him in surprise.

"Why don't you take one of the Council's pickups and go to Arrowhead?" the Judge asked. "It will do you good."

Joe lay awake a long time after he went to bed.

Seven

The air seemed different on the other side of the gate. It smelled different. It tasted different. It was like cold water. It was frightening.

Joe drove the little pickup on the dirt road that led out of the reservation. He stopped at the state highway. There was a stop sign and he had to stop but he waited longer than he had to before he could bring himself to turn left on the highway to Arrowhead.

He felt he was doing something wrong. He felt he was doing something illegal. It was a crazy feeling. There was no reason he could not leave the reservation and the truck had been loaned to him by the Council. But he felt guilty. He thought about it, sitting behind the wheel of the pickup, the highway empty for as far as he could see in both directions. He thought about it for a long while, breathing the air that was different from the reservation air. Finally he knew what he felt. He felt like he was going AWOL.

That was the craziest feeling of all. And yet that was the way he felt. He would not have been surprised if the MPs pulled up in jeeps and hauled him in.

He turned into the highway. The feeling stayed with him in the open country with the harsh, coarse earth and the grotesque cacti, some of it in summer blossom still. He never got over the sight of cactus in flower. Most cactus was something tough and hard and ornery to him and then in the spring some of it produced flowers and even the flowers seemed embarrassed.

He drove slowly and he tried to stop thinking that he was escaping from someplace, that he was doing what he shouldn't be doing. He had been home only three weeks or so and the reservation had already done its job of closing in.

After a while he thought about that less. He let himself enjoy the little things of driving. He accelerated and braked and followed the contours of the road. He passed a car and then was passed. All of that occupied his hands and feet and his eyes and his mind.

It wasn't that he liked to drive so much and it wasn't that driving this old heap was anything. It was that he could put himself together again. He could concentrate on something that made demands. He drove much slower than the speed limit. He made turns carefully and gauged his braking when he came to intersections. He began to feel good. The hard country was close to him.

The speed he was driving made the trip to Arrowhead almost two hours. When he saw the outskirts of the town he slowed even more. He had been to Arrowhead a couple of times with his father years before but he had never been there alone. To Joe it was a strange place. He realized he had been driving slowly for more reasons than one. He had wanted to delay his arrival at this strange place.

The town started with a gas station and then there was another gas station on the other side of the road and then there was a saloon and then there were some stores and then a couple of motels. After that there were a couple of more stores and more gas stations and then the open country again and another forty or fifty miles to the next town.

He drove slowly into the town. In some ways he would have felt more at home entering a village in Viet Nam. Entering a village in Nam was part of a process that he had a part in and he could take that in stride. This was different. The people here were enemies too but the rules were different and unspoken.

He parked the truck and got down. He was wearing his

best army shirt and pants. He could have put on levis and a checkered shirt but he chose the army clothes. He told himself they were the cleanest and best. That wasn't the whole reason. They also were protection.

He walked the length of the town and started back. He thought about stopping at one of the bars for a beer. Once Indians couldn't buy anything with alcohol in it. Once Indians couldn't even buy a cup of coffee in a place that sold anything with alcohol. Now they could. But he couldn't get himself to go inside a saloon. It was enough to be an Indian on the street, even an Indian dressed like a soldier. He couldn't be an Indian at a bar.

He went into one of the cafes. He ordered ham and eggs and toast and coffee. The food tasted good. Nobody looked at him in any special way and the waitress treated him like anybody else.

When he was finished and was drinking the last of his coffee he noticed a cigarette machine and he thought about buying a pack. He decided he was going to stay off. He had made up his mind about that. You weren't much if you went back and forth about things.

He went out into the street. The sun was high now and it was hot and he felt good. His belly was filled and he felt free. He didn't have that AWOL feeling anymore. He didn't feel altogether comfortable in this strange town but he didn't feel he was breaking any law.

He walked down the street and he saw a store that sold clothing. He went inside. There was a man behind a counter. He was small and he had a little moustache and he wore glasses. He asked Joe if he could help him. Joe said he'd like to look around. The man said, fine, take his time. Joe did. He looked at everything. He had to. It was something born in him. He had to see everything first. He would have liked to just point to this and that but he couldn't do it.

He finally picked out some levis and some shirts and some white sox and a pair of heavy shoes. As he was selecting them the small man with the moustache followed him and took the things from him. Joe wondered at first whether the man was afraid he was going to try to steal something but then he thought that maybe the man was being polite and taking the things away so Joe could have his hands free to pick out something else.

Joe had his feelers out for the man. He was ready for any kind of attitude. He would not have been surprised if the man had asked him to show his money before he started selling him anything. But the man just waited on him and he even suggested that he get shirts a size larger because they'd probably shrink.

"They always say they won't shrink but they always do," the man said.

Joe thought it was good of the man to take that interest. He paid for everything and the man wrapped it up and tied it with a string and put a little wooden handle on the string. He hefted the package.

"I think that'll hold, Sergeant," he said.

Joe went out of the store feeling better than he had for some time. He put the package into the truck and went into a general store. He bought some goods for his family. Staples, canned food, potatoes, some tobacco for his father. He stayed in the store a long time looking at the prices for everything. He remembered Linton's prices and some of the good feeling went away.

He paid for the groceries and carried the carton out to the truck. That about did it. He thought again about having a beer but he decided against it. They probably wouldn't treat him in an ordinary way in a saloon. He didn't want to wipe away all the good feeling.

He started out of town. He saw something he had missed

before. A used-car lot. What stopped him was the sign, THE
TWO VETS. He pulled up to the curb and looked over the lot.
A man came out of a small shack and walked over to him.

"Looking for anything, Sarge?" the man asked, looking
him over.

"No," Joe said.

"Come on over and have a good look, Sarge," the man
said. "Won't cost you nothing."

After a moment Joe got down from the truck. The man led
him into the lot. The man wore boots and Western clothes
and a big hat. He was fat and he needed a shave and he had
a stub of a cigar in his mouth. The cigar was unlit. He followed Joe around the lot. Joe passed the used passenger cars
and went over to where the small trucks were parked.

"Looking for a pickup?" the man asked.

"I don't know," Joe said. He didn't know why he was
there.

"Got a couple of beauties sitting around."

Joe asked, "Why is this place called THE TWO VETS?"

"Me and my partner. He was navy. I was army."

"Where?"

"Viet Nam. Got back a year ago." He looked around the
lot. His face was proud, even with the cigar stump in his
mouth. "Got this going since then. It ain't a hell of a lot but
it's something." He turned his eyes to Joe. "You just out,
Sarge?"

"Yes," Joe said.

"From where?"

"Same place you were."

"I'll be damned," the man said. He put out a big hand.
"Welcome back, Sarge."

Joe took the hand.

The man looked at him more closely. "You an Indian?"

Joe nodded. He felt a small tingling go through him.

35

"From San Pedro?" the man asked.

"Yes."

Joe started back for his pickup.

The man followed him. "What's your hurry, Sarge?" he asked.

Joe moved faster. He had to get away from there. He had to get away from the fat man with the cigar stub. He had to get back into the truck and then back to the reservation.

"What's your name, Sarge?" the fat man asked.

Joe could hear him behind him. He could hear the fat man breathing hard. He would have liked a gun in his hands. He would have felt safer with an army gun.

"Don't rush away, Sarge," the man said from very close behind him.

Joe whirled around. He didn't want to be jumped. If there was going to be a fight he wanted to face the enemy. He didn't want a shiv in his back.

He spread his legs a little and braced himself. The man puffed to a stop. The man laughed.

"I guess I'm out of shape," he said. "Don't eat me out."

Joe stood there, his arms half bent, his hands ready for anything.

The man tried to catch his breath. "Don't look at me that way, Sarge. I never got past PFC and that kind of look scares the hell out of me."

After a moment Joe relaxed. He smiled.

"This lard," the fat man said. "It keeps piling on. Business is lousy. Nothing to do but sit around and drink beer. Say, Sarge, would you like a cold beer?"

"No," Joe said.

He went on to his pickup. He climbed up. The man leaned at the window.

"You need a truck, you come back, hear?"

Joe nodded. What had made him look at trucks? Why would he buy a truck?

36

"I got some clean ones, Sarge," the fat man said. He took a card out of his shirt pocket and gave it to Joe.

Joe looked at it. He saw THE TWO VETS and in the corner the name, Al Adams.

"This is a crooked racket, Sarge," Al Adams said. "But I wouldn't screw anybody who's been over in that lousy place."

Joe started the truck and drove out of town. He'd gone about five miles when he stopped and pulled over to the side of the road. He looked at the gray hills and the cactus. He saw a jackrabbit. A lot of thoughts ran through his head. He tried to straighten them out. They were new thoughts and he had to think on them slowly.

He turned the truck around and drove back to Arrowhead. He stopped in front of the general store. He sat in the truck for several minutes. He was shaking just a little. He was thinking a new course and it didn't come easily. Apaches like to talk a lot about things with each other before making a move but he had nobody to talk to.

He remembered that back in Nam he was reckoned to be a guy with a fair share of guts. He summoned those guts now.

He got down and went into the general store. He talked to the little man with the moustache. He went back to the used-car lot. He talked to Al Adams.

Joe told both men that he had some thinking to do and maybe he'd get back to them. Then he returned to San Pedro.

Eight

About a week later the Deputy Agent, Bill Hunter, was crossing the parade ground around which the official buildings were grouped. He saw Joe Murdock coming out of the Tribal Council building.

The area was still called "the parade ground." In the old days when the reservation was run by the army the soldiers marched and drilled and held retreat there. No military had been around for more than half a century but the Agent Lawton was a believer in tradition and insisted it still be called "the parade ground."

Even from a distance Hunter thought he could see a spring in Joe's walk. He waved to him and they said hello and Hunter asked, "How about a cup of coffee?"

They went into the commissary. They sat down with the coffee and Hunter offered Joe a cigarette. Joe told him he had quit.

"What's been happening with you?" Hunter asked.

"I've been busy."

"Is that so?"

Joe put a spoonful of sugar into his coffee and stirred it slowly. "I had this idea," he said. He wanted to talk about it but it was not easy to talk about it, especially to a white man. But he had a feeling that he might trust this white man. And that was odd, because when they first met they had opposed each other.

"You did?"

"You know how I feel about that thief Linton."

"I know."

"I had this idea."

38

Hunter nodded. He sipped his coffee.

"It looks like it might work," Joe said.

"Good."

"You see, there's a used-car dealer in Arrowhead. He was in Nam."

Hunter nodded.

"He has this pickup there. It's in good shape."

"I heard something about all this," Hunter said.

Joe looked up swiftly. A wary look passed over his face. His eyes got careful. "The Agent knows about it?"

"Is there any reason he should not?"

"No."

"He doesn't like the idea?" Joe said. All the feelers were out now. He was dealing with the enemy again.

"He thinks it's a big thing," Hunter said.

"For an Indian."

"For anybody without experience."

Joe finished his coffee and got another. He poured milk into it and stirred in sugar. "What does he say?" He told himself he really didn't give a damn what the Agent might say or think, but he knew he was lying to himself. "What does he know?"

Hunter shrugged. "He heard that you're trying to get some Indians to go in with you buying this truck."

"What else?"

"That you're trying to form some kind of cooperative, to buy goods for Indians in Arrowhead."

"Is that against the law?" Joe demanded, suddenly angry.

"In no way."

"Then why is the Agent against it?"

"I didn't say that."

"I know he is!" Joe said loudly. When Hunter didn't answer, he asked, more quietly, "What do you think?"

"You seem to be going about it the right way," Hunter

said. "Beyond that I don't know." He looked at Joe for a moment. "What are you going to get out of this? If this works out it's going to take a lot of your time."

Joe nodded. "I haven't worked out all the details. But I've told the people that if this is successful it will become a full-time job and that I'd have to make a living for myself. Everybody understands that. What I'll have to do is work out the costs of the payments on the truck and the upkeep and gas and so on and add on to that what's fair to me."

Hunter asked, "Why do you want to do this?"

"How can you ask me that? You know why."

"Why, Joe," Hunter said. "Why do you want to do this?"

"The sutler is robbing us."

"Is that the only reason?"

Joe frowned and thought. After a while he said, "We never stole from each other, never. It was something we never did. In the old days we stole from everybody else. Apart from hunting that was how we made our living. But inside the tribe we never stole from each other. We were all one. It would have been like stealing from yourself."

He was silent again. These were old thoughts but he had never tried to put them into words. Now he was putting them into words and for a white man.

"This is supposed to be us," he said, waving his hand to take in the reservation. "It says so in the treaties. You are supposed to look after us. You are supposed to teach us, like wise uncles. We are told that you know best about everything. You are supposed to see that nobody cheats us. But do you do that? No. You let our money be stolen from us. The people work hard for their money and they are poor and you let it be stolen. Just as though someone with a gun took pennies and nickels and dimes out of the people's pockets."

He drank some of his coffee. He cupped his hands around the thick mug as though it were cold and he needed warmth.

"In Nam, sometimes I felt like I was the white man and the Vietnamese were Indians. They were the natives there and they belonged there and they were getting shoved and hurt and killed and their homes were destroyed. And we were wearing American uniforms and we were supposed to be there to help them and protect them but we were the ones who pushed and hurt and killed and destroyed. I've thought about that. Now I understand I should not be surprised the army did that. I've learned about Camp Grant and Wounded Knee and other places, lots of other places. That was done by the army against the natives here. That's what I think, Mr. Hunter. I think the army loused up that little country, Viet Nam, the way the army loused up lots of places. Only this time I had a part in it and I did what I was ordered to do and I know it will take a long time for those people to get over us. It was done to the Indians more than a hundred years ago and we haven't got over it yet."

He was silent again. Then he said, "Maybe that's why I want to do something here. Not only because they're my own people who are getting pushed around but because maybe it will make up a little for what I did to those poor bastards over there." He stood up. "I have to go to Arrowhead."

Hunter mashed out his cigarette.

"It isn't just Linton," Joe said. "It's the fact that he's allowed to get away with it. All of you people know about it and you let him get away with it. Can you understand that, Mr. Hunter?"

Hunter nodded slowly.

Joe walked out of the commissary, his back straight, his head held high. Hunter watched him go.

Three days later when Joe returned from another trip to Arrowhead he was arrested by one of the Apache policemen on charges brought against him by the Agent.

Nine

The trial of Joe Murdock on charges of threatening the person and property of Thaddeus Linton was held in the courtroom of the Tribal Council building two evenings later. Judge Moore presided.

Word had got round the reservation fast. The chamber was filled early.

Some of the white Bureau personnel were present as well as Indians. No one could remember the last time charges were preferred by the Agent himself. Some said it had never happened before.

Oliver and Florence Murdock were among the first to arrive. They wanted to be sitting there to be seen by everybody else who managed to get inside the courtroom. They wanted everybody to know they were not ashamed of their son.

Mrs. Murdock wore her best Mother Hubbard, the dress style settled on by Apache women a century before, soon after they moved onto reservations. Oliver Murdock wore levis and a black and red checkered shirt. He had a kerchief around his neck, held by a silver and turquoise loop. Both he and Mrs. Murdock bowed their heads gravely to people who spoke to them or who nodded.

Jennie Gates was there and she tried to hide her fear but it was there to see. Linton was there to testify, as was Deputy Agent Hunter. Hunter sat next to his wife, Winnie, a plump, matronly woman. Lawton was not there but no one expected he would be.

In any case there was no need for him to be there. Lester Matthews was a member of the Tribal Council and a powerful force. He was also one of the very few Apaches who was close to the Agent. Lester Matthews said often that Townsend Lawton was the finest agent in the entire Indian Bureau and that San Pedro was lucky to have him. The Agent had stated publicly that he considered Lester Matthews the wisest and most competent man on the Council. Everybody in the room knew that Matthews was there as the eyes and ears of the Agent.

There was a stir in the room as Joe was led in by an Apache policeman. Joe was wearing the new levis and shirt and shoes he had bought for himself in Arrowhead. He had not been confined since his arrest, only ordered to remain on the reservation. He had stayed at home, mostly in his room. Neither his mother nor father had talked much about the arrest. Judge Moore had not visited the house during that time.

Joe looked down at the floor as he entered and took the defendant's chair. He was embarrassed at being on public display. He had asked permission to face Judge Moore in private. The request had been denied. Everything had to be open and aboveboard.

A few minutes later Judge Moore appeared and sat down on the rostrum. Some of the older Apaches started to get to their feet but the Judge waved them down. He ordered Joe to rise and face him and he told him in plain words what he had been accused of.

"Do you have anything to say for yourself?" the Judge asked.

"No," Joe answered.

"How do you plead? Guilty or not guilty?"

"Not guilty."

Judge Moore told Joe to sit down and he called upon Linton.

Linton stood up and shuffled to the center of the courtroom. He pointed a finger at Joe. "That man threatened me.

He accused me of being dishonest. He was going to break up my store and then commit bodily harm upon me. I tell you, until Mr. Hunter put some sense into him I feared for my life."

He drew breath. He was a little man and he looked forlorn. He told the Judge how he had spent almost all his life providing for the needs of the Chiricahua people.

"I'm a poor man," he said. "I have always been fair to my customers. Despite that this wild man was going to destroy my property and injure me."

The Apache spectators kept straight faces. They were all used to hiding their feelings. That was part of their blood.

Joe looked at Linton and listened to him without any expression at all. He did not draw back when the sutler jabbed a finger at him, almost touching him.

Linton was prepared to go on for some time, repeating himself, when Judge Moore rapped his gavel. Linton subsided and sat down.

Two or three of the Indians who had been in the store when Joe had acted up were now questioned by the Judge. They did not give much. They said they were occupied looking at merchandise when all this took place. The Judge did not press them. He called the Deputy Agent.

Hunter told the story as he remembered it. When he was finished the Judge leaned forward.

"Mr. Hunter, you heard Mr. Linton testify that his life was in danger. Can you substantiate that?"

"I didn't hear any personal threats," Hunter said.

"When you said, 'Knock it off, Sergeant,' what exactly did you mean?"

"That's an old army expression, Judge," Hunter said.

"I know that. But how did you intend it to be taken?"

"You know, take it easy, shut up, cut it out."

"Cut out what?"

44

"Oh, anything."

"When you made that remark to the defendant he was not speaking to Mr. Linton, was he?"

"No."

"Then when you used the expression you did not mean for him to shut up."

"I guess not."

"Then you anticipated the defendant was about to commit an act of violence and you used the clever device of using an army expression the defendant would recognize to stop him."

Hunter thought for a moment. "Judge Moore, I don't know what Joe Murdock intended to do. I saw him standing there and Linton was as sore as a grizzly and he was screaming at Joe and waving his fist at him and I reckoned anything might happen. Linton could have picked up something and hit Joe on the head. Joe could have taken a swing at Linton. I said the first thing that came to my mind to stop anything."

"But you addressed yourself to the defendant."

"Yes."

"You did not consider it was Mr. Linton who needed primarily to be restrained."

"Maybe not," Hunter said after a little bit.

"Mr. Linton has testified that the defendant was about to push the counter over on him and that even after you prevented the defendant from doing that he pushed the counter a little bit anyway as to show Mr. Linton what he had had in mind. Will you corroborate that?"

"I have no idea what Joe Murdock had in mind."

Judge Moore leaned forward again. "As a witness to the event do you believe Mr. Linton was justified in the fear he has expressed here?"

Hunter hesitated again. "I think Linton is the only one who can judge that."

"Mr. Hunter, did you see the defendant tip that counter toward Mr. Linton?"

Hunter nodded. "I believe he did."

"Thank you, Mr. Hunter, you may stand down." Then Judge Moore said, "Will the defendant please rise."

Joe stood up.

"Now that you have heard the testimony of the plaintiff and the witnesses is there anything you would like to say."

"No," Joe said. He felt terrible standing there with everybody looking at him and all he wanted was for this to get over so he could be alone.

"Consider that again," Judge Moore said.

Joe pressed his lips hard. All he could see was Judge Moore looking down at him but he could feel all the eyes on his back.

"Do you still deny the charges made against you?" the Judge asked.

Joe said nothing.

The Judge tried again. "Am I to base my verdict on what was brought out in court? Have you no wish at all to speak in your own behalf?"

Joe looked inside himself for his place to retreat but this time he could not find it. And he knew the reason he could not find it was because he had tainted himself in the courtroom. He had tainted himself by lying.

What made it worse was that he had lied before the enemy. Judge Moore was an old family friend but at this moment he was the enemy. Linton was always the enemy. The Agent, represented by Lester Matthews, was the enemy. Hunter was the enemy. There were others in the room. He had, he knew, to purify himself.

"I would have done it," he said. He heard some murmuring behind him but he did not feel embarrassed.

"You would have done what?" the Judge asked.

"I would have pushed the counter over."

"I told you!" Linton yelled.

Judge Moore pounded his gavel. "Go on, Joe."

"If Mr. Hunter hadn't stopped me I would have done that," Joe said. He could feel the eyes on his back but he didn't mind now.

"Is there anything else?" the Judge asked.

"Yes, there is something else. After I pushed over the counter I might have done more."

"Against the person of Mr. Linton?" Judge Moore asked.

"Yes." Joe had himself again. He had his strength and he was not afraid of anything. He heard the low whispering behind him and he could hear Linton mumbling to someone but he was not afraid of any of that.

"Is that all of it?" Judge Moore asked.

"No. There is something else. A question."

"Ask your question."

"All of this happened in the sutler's store more than a month ago. My question is why Agent Lawton waited until now to bring his charges."

"That is no part of this procedure," the Judge said.

"I suppose not," Joe said. "All of you set your own rules and nobody is supposed to ask why." He felt he was cleansing himself with each word. "I wonder whether the Agent and the sutler brought the charges now, at this time, because I was trying to start a business in competition with the sutler."

Now the voices rose in the courtroom and Judge Moore had to pound his gavel several times. "I have no way of knowing," he said, when he had restored quiet.

"No," Joe said. "Nobody knows anything. Nobody knows anything he doesn't want to know."

Presently Judge Moore said in an even voice, "Joe, your admission of your guilt simplifies matters. Perhaps it would have been better if you made that admission sooner."

Joe was silent. He couldn't explain that he could not have

made it sooner. He had had to work it out of himself. He could respect himself again but he did not have to give any more.

Judge Moore tapped his gavel lightly. "Joe Murdock, you have admitted the truth of the charges brought against you. This court sentences you to thirty days in jail, sentence to commence immediately. This case is closed."

The Apache policeman walked over to Joe. He did not put his hand on him. Without looking at anyone, Joe walked out the back door of the courtroom. He heard Linton say to someone, "Scot-free. He got off almost scot-free."

Ten

The early morning sun poked fingers through the bars and woke Joe up.

The cell, in the back part of the Council building, was small. It contained a cot, a small table and a straight-backed chair. There was no toilet. The prisoner had to call for the guard to go to the toilet.

It was very early in the morning. From the one barred window Joe could see a part of the parade ground. There was no one about. He had to go to the toilet but he thought maybe the guard was still asleep and he did not want to disturb him. He could wait.

The Apache policeman who had led Joe to the cell the night before told him he had gotten off easy, just as Linton had said he had. The policeman had said he could have been put behind bars for six months or maybe even more for getting set to beat up on a white man. Fighting between Indians was different. That was acceptable. That was expected. But not against whites.

Joe didn't mind being in the cell. He knew he had been on the verge of something violent there in Linton's store and he knew you could commit violence only when it was official policy, as in war. He knew, too, that there were worse kinds of punishment than either imprisonment or death. But the whites didn't know much about that. Shaming a person was worse than putting him behind bars. Taking away his dignity was worse.

Jail was nothing. Thirty days was nothing. Maybe that was because the whole reservation was a jail. No, it wasn't that.

Lying on the cot, listening for some sounds from the guard, Joe knew it wasn't that. The jail was inside himself. He knew he deserved to be punished.

After a while he heard footsteps and the guard appeared. He was an old Apache and he carried a tray with coffee and some bread. Joe thanked him and said he would have to go to the toilet first.

The guard unlocked the cell door. "Don't run away," he said.

"I won't."

"Come back quickly. My wife made the coffee and it will get cold and it will not be fair to her."

"I will," Joe promised.

After breakfast he stood at the window and looked out and saw life starting on the reservation. People were going into the administration building, most of them whites. He thought he could make out Jennie Gates but he was not sure.

He could see the people but unless they walked over to the jail they could not see him. That was good. He did not want to be seen. He did not want anybody to visit him. He remembered feeling this way the two times he had been wounded in Nam. Some of his friends came to the field hospital to see how he was. He knew they had done that out of friendship and concern and he did not want to be rude but he wished they had not come. Sickness, a wound, was a private thing. That's the way he felt right now.

He had to work out some kind of plan for himself for the thirty days. A routine of some sort. Not that time was a problem. Time meant little. There had always been days and days with nothing happening. Idleness meant less to him than to a white. White men got restless. He did not.

But he did not want to waste thirty days entirely. Thirty days were thirty days of his life.

He thought he should do some exercises. He would be pretty much confined to that little room and he ought to keep his body in shape. He owed it to his body. His body had served him. It had never let him down. Even after he had been wounded it served him until the medics could take over.

He remembered the old army setting-up exercises. He started doing push-ups and sit-ups and he stretched and twisted and bent. The old prison guard came to pick up the breakfast tray and he watched Joe for a while. He walked away shaking his head. It looked silly to him.

When Joe was finished with his exercising he sat down. It was still morning. There was a long day ahead. He started to think about the business he had been trying to get started. He wondered what would happen to that. He wondered whether everything would hold still for thirty days.

He heard someone at the cell door. The guard unlocked the door. It was one of the reservation missionaries come to pay him a visit.

Joe stood up and greeted the missionary who was a small man with tufts of white hair that grew on his head without any design. Joe had no desire to see the missionary but he had to be polite. Apaches had never paid much attention to missionaries, not the way some other Indian tribes had and so the missionary didn't have much to do on the reservation and this was a worthy event in his life. Joe knew he had to respect that.

The missionary asked him whether he was comfortable and was there anything he wanted.

"Something to read," Joe said.

The missionary nodded and smiled nervously. Missionaries were always uncertain with Apaches. They had not dared to try to convert Apaches when they were still free. It was only when the Apaches allowed themselves to be put on a reservation that the missionaries had come in. By then it was very late and the Apaches listened, but did not pay much attention.

"I brought you some reading material," the missionary

51

said, happy that he had anticipated this. He had a rich voice, coming from such a shy-looking person.

The missionary opened a large manila envelope and took out some pamphlets. Joe looked at them. They were religious tracts. Then the missionary took a small Bible from his coat pocket.

None of this was what Joe had wanted but he would not let the missionary know that. He had to let the missionary retain his good thought. The missionary chatted for a while about nothing and said he would drop in again and Joe thanked him and the missionary left.

Joe looked at his watch. He had eaten and had exercised and had had a visitor and it was just after ten o'clock.

A little later the old guard brought him some lunch, some kind of stew, and then Joe stretched out on the cot and stared at the ceiling until he heard footsteps, not the steps of the guard alone but of another person as well, and he looked at the door and saw it was Sam Hopkins. He lived near Joe's father's house.

Sam was a big man with a long horse face. He always looked sad but he was not a sad man.

Sam sat down on the chair and smoked a cigarette. He said Joe's parents were okay. He said it as though Joe were far away and had not heard from his parents for some time. Joe said he was glad to hear that and to please tell his parents that he was okay too.

Then Sam Hopkins said, "I've been talking to some of the men."

Joe didn't have to ask him what men. He knew Sam meant the men with whom he had talked about going into business.

"They don't feel the same way now," Sam Hopkins said.

Joe nodded. Of course they wouldn't feel the same way. Joe had lost face and that made a difference.

"You can't blame them," Sam Hopkins said. He was trou-

52

bled to have to bring this information and yet he was performing an act of friendship.

"I don't blame them," Joe said.

"Maybe later on," Sam Hopkins said.

"Maybe," Joe said. He knew they were both lying. There would be no later on. Joe knew he had a label on himself now. He was a loser. The Agent had personally singled him out. Everybody got the message. The Agent had won. Even the jail sentence didn't matter. He could be let out of the cell that day and it wouldn't matter one way or the other. The Agent had won.

Sam Hopkins asked him if he could bring him anything and Joe said no. Sam Hopkins said he would drop in again and he left.

Joe lay down on the cot and stared at the ceiling again. He was not surprised the men had walked away from him. That was the way things were. You could make all kinds of sounds and have all kinds of schemes but in the end the whites won. They had their own establishment and the Apaches had their establishment and they formed a front and you couldn't lick them. It was a law of life and Joe did not feel bitter about it. It was silly to feel bitter about what could not be changed. He thought for a little while longer how nice it would have been if his plans had worked out and then he put the thoughts out of his mind because they were now without meaning.

The days went by. He set himself a routine that went beyond morning exercises. It made everything easier when there was a schedule. The army had drilled that into him. Keep men busy. Good or bad it was better than nothing.

The missionary visited him a couple of more times. To please him Joe read the religious tracts. Sam Hopkins visited him again and brought him some paperbacks. Sam Hopkins had a sense of humor, Joe decided. Sam brought him paperbacks about the West, about fights between white men and Indians. It was Sam's little joke and Joe appreciated it.

Joe's parents did not visit him, neither did his brother or sister. That was good. Joe knew his mother probably wanted very much to visit him and maybe his sister did too but he knew his father would not permit that. His father knew about things. Even though some of his manhood had been taken away in the accident his father was still a man and knew about the right things. So did his brother. To have visited him, to have seen him a prisoner confined to a small room, guarded by an armed man, would have taken away some of his own manhood in the eyes of his family.

Every couple of days the guard on duty brought him clean laundry and took away the used laundry. That clean laundry was a message from his mother to him. There was no need for her to come in person.

Jennie Gates had visited him on the second day. He told her not to come again.

"I don't want you to," he said.

"I waited one day," she said.

"Thank you for that. But please don't come again."

"Why not?" She did not show her hurt.

She should know, he thought. He was trapped there, an animal in a cage, and he didn't want to be seen there except maybe by somebody who didn't count, like the missionary, or somebody like Sam Hopkins who made jokes.

"Don't come again," he said. Now he saw the hurt in her eyes but he could not help that.

For a little while she didn't say anything. She stood there looking at nothing. She didn't know what to do or what to say. He watched and he felt terrible.

"I thought you would like to see me," she said finally, but the tone in her voice belied her.

How could he explain? How could he tell her how much he

54

liked to see her at the right times. How could he explain this was the wrongest time. He could explain all right but how could he do it without making that hurt in her face worse. He could stand almost anything except to see that hurt.

She turned and started out of the cell.

"Jennie," he said.

She stopped as though she had been given a reprieve.

"Jennie," he said to her back. It was a little easier talking to her back. He couldn't see the hurt on her back. "Jennie," he said again. It wasn't so easy after all.

"You're proud," she said, still not turning. "It's that you're proud. You don't have to tell me anything, Joe." She turned and now her face was calm. "I should be beholden to you, Joe. Your mother and father know you don't want them to see you here because they're close to you. And now you make me part of that too. I'm beholden to you, Joe."

He wanted to say something or maybe just touch her but he couldn't do either and looking at her face he knew it wasn't necessary. She looked at him and he wanted to laugh and cry at the same time and then she left.

She did not come again. Once the missionary brought his wife. She was a small woman, like a bird. She seemed frightened. The missionary brought her in triumph, to show her he was accepted by the Apache prisoner. The missionary asked Joe, for the first time, whether he wanted to pray together with him and his wife. Joe said no.

The missionary's wife asked, "Would you like us to fall upon our knees and pray for you?" She had a bird's voice, chirpy.

Joe wished he could have said yes. "No," he said.

The missionary nodded gravely. "I can understand that, Joe, but perhaps you won't object if we pray for you when we get back to the mission."

Joe didn't answer that.

The month went on. Joe thought about a lot of things. He had the time. He thought about the Deputy Agent. He felt no anger for what Hunter had said in the courtroom. If the Deputy Agent had not spoken as he had Joe would have lost respect for him.

He had one surprise visitor, Judge Moore. The Judge said right away that this was an official visit, to make certain everything was in order. Joe didn't know whether that was entirely true, but it was a delicate matter and he accepted it.

It was the first time Joe had spoken to Judge Moore since the courtroom trial. He asked him to explain how things had happened, chiefly why the Agent had taken so long to bring the charges.

"You asked me that in the courtroom," Judge Moore said.

"You didn't answer."

"I didn't know the answer."

"Do you know the answer now?"

"No."

They talked some more. Joe asked questions and the Judge explained that the Agent had presented the charges to the Council, and that the councilmen had to decide whether or not to act upon them. That interested Joe.

"You mean they could have dumped the charges?" he asked.

"Technically, yes."

"Technically? What does that mean?"

"According to the Tribal Charter they can act or not act on charges presented to them as they see fit."

"They saw fit."

"Yes."

Joe thought about that. "They tell me I'm the first prisoner they've had here in more than three months."

"I believe that's right."

"There are more than four thousand people on the San Pedro Reservation."

"I believe that's right too."

"We must be a tribe of saints," Joe said.

Judge Moore did not say anything.

"Or else the Council usually doesn't see fit."

The Judge looked uncomfortable.

"Maybe the Council sees fit usually when the Agent wants it to see fit," Joe said. He still did not feel bitter. That was the way things were.

Judge Moore got to his feet. "I'm sorry you feel that way, Joe," he said and left.

On the thirtieth day Joe was released. He was let out early in the morning, just after dawn, long before the parade ground came to life. Nobody saw him leave jail. He felt no sudden sense of freedom as he walked away.

Eleven

Joe loosened the girth and pulled the saddle off the horse. He hefted the saddle onto the top rung of the corral fence. He went back to the horse and took off the blanket and slapped the animal on the rump. The horse whinnied and wandered over to the feed trough.

Joe folded the blanket and put it next to the saddle. He straightened and rubbed his back. He had not ridden this much for years. The insides of his legs were sore and his bottom was sore and his back ached. He felt tired but good.

He stretched. The Council wasn't so dumb, he thought. He had hardly been out of jail before they rounded him up and sent him to the range to ride herd on the tribal cattle.

They must have thought that after the stretch in the clink he would come out full of anger, ready to do something against somebody, the Agent, or Linton. And so they had shipped him out to the range on the other side of the reservation to get him away and take some of the starch out of him. They were wrong in their thinking this time, of course. He wouldn't have done anything. But what they did was smart. It showed him that the Council was concerned with more than just getting along with the white authorities. They also had some thoughts about the Apache people they represented. He had ridden hard all day and even though his body was unused to that it had felt good to have a horse between his legs, to smell the hot ammonia smell of horse sweat, to hear the creak of leather and the thud of hooves, to feel the country around him. He had been assigned to round up strays. He had forgotten how pure the land was, harsh, hard,

58

unyielding and pure. He had collected his strays, and he had watched the other men rope up the animals for branding. It was all good. It was fresh and away and good.

Suddenly he saw his father limping toward him, carrying the big, black tally book. It was like punching a time clock except Oliver Murdock took every man's word on the hours he put in. He did not check. He did not believe anyone would lie.

Joe told his father how long he had worked that day, and his father wrote down his name and the number of hours.

Other men drifted in and unsaddled their horses and then reported to his father. Joe, sitting down, his back against a tree trunk, wondered how it had been when his father was one of the men who came in and reported to the tally keeper. He wondered whether his father was bitter about the accident.

He watched his father now, wetting the tip of the stubby pencil and putting down numbers after names.

The wind shifted and he smelled the beef being cooked over an open fire. The cook was another man who had been hurt on the range. There was nothing wrong with being a cook but Joe was glad his father was the tally keeper and not the cook.

The dinner was good, beef and beans and bread and hot, strong coffee. The men sat around and talked. The men asked Joe different things and the atmosphere was good and he answered them. He talked more about Nam than he had since his return. The men listened and were respectful.

Afterwards some of the men saddled up and rode home. Others spread blankets and went to sleep near the fire. Oliver Murdock told Joe they would stay on the range that night. That was okay with Joe. He liked sleeping in the open.

His father filled his pipe and lit it. "How do you feel?"

"Okay."

"Sore?"

"A little."

"You'll get used to it."

There was nothing special in his father's voice so maybe Joe only imagined his father would like to have some of that soreness, that good tired feeling.

"I never knew we had so many beeves," Joe said.

"It's a good herd."

"It seems strange."

"Raising beef?"

Joe nodded.

Oliver Murdock chuckled. He relit his pipe. "It would have seemed strange to your great-grandfather. The only beef he ever had was when he raised an animal out of some white rancher's herd."

"How did we get started? Most other Indian tribes out here still don't breed cattle."

Oliver Murdock puffed on his pipe. The firelight flickered on his seamed face. "Cochise started it. You know about Cochise."

"Everybody knows about Cochise."

"You didn't know he started this."

"No, I didn't," Joe admitted.

"Then you don't know about Cochise. What do you know about him?"

"He made peace with the white man and then he was screwed. Everybody knows that."

Oliver pulled on his pipe. "Maybe so. Maybe that says it." He was silent for a while. "The thing to remember is that we never were defeated. We were tricked afterward but we never were defeated. Did you know that?"

"There are different ways to be defeated. I know that," Joe said.

Oliver Murdock shook his head slowly. "In a war there is only one way. What happens after that is something dif-

60

ferent. What happened to us afterward was bad. But we were not defeated in the fighting. The President of the United States, he was General Grant and an important soldier, realized the army could not defeat Cochise and he sent another famous general out here to find Cochise and to beg him to make peace. The United States asked for peace, not Cochise."

It pleased Joe to hear his father talking about those old times. His father seemed strong now. He was not walking and not having to favor his bad leg and his voice was low and strong and he knew things.

"Cochise beat the army every time," Oliver said. "He broke the reputation of one famous general after another. They all came out here with big names from the Civil War and Cochise broke them, one after the other. They finally quit. The United States quit. President Grant sent a big war hero, a general with one arm, out here to ask Cochise to please stop fighting."

"What good did that do?" Joe asked.

"It did good," Oliver said. "Cochise was winning the fighting, yes, but he had a vision. He knew that the white men were coming out here more and more, like leaves on the trees, like grains of sand on the desert, and he had the vision that in the end there would be defeat and death for the Apache. He knew even while he was winning that in the end he would lose. So he made peace. And he kept it. The Apache never broke his word. The white man broke his. That is something to remember."

Joe didn't say anything.

Oliver Murdock waved his hand. "We were supposed to be given our own land, the land we had always had, but after Cochise died they betrayed us and moved us up here. They waited until he died and then they did it. They wanted our land because they thought it was better than this land.

"The government did strange things. We had always eaten

61

corn we got from Mexicans and Navajos and we did not know what wheat was but they sent us wheat and we did not know what to do with it. They did not give us blankets and clothing. It seems they wanted us to rise up and make trouble so they could kill us. But we did not rise up. Cochise had said we would not and we honored his word in his death as we had in his life."

There was quiet pride in Oliver Murdock's voice. Without looking at Joe, he said, "You know something about that. You know something about truth. You know truth is the strongest thing there is."

It was Oliver Murdock's first reference to Joe's confession in the courtroom. Oliver had said nothing to Joe about his time in jail until now.

Joe felt the tingle under his skin.

"We did not know how to plant things," Oliver went on. "When Cochise made the peace we knew nothing about those things. That was when Cochise said we would raise beef. The people laughed. Some of the men were angry. They said they would never be grandmothers to cows. Cochise told them the white men raised cattle and that the people knew from experience that the white men were not women.

"The people said they would try. The white ranchers sent up some cattle to get them started. They didn't send up the cattle because they were good-hearted or generous. They were happy the Apaches weren't fighting and stealing any more and they were happy the Apaches wanted to raise their own beef. The ranchers knew that would make their own cattle safer."

Joe noticed now that some of the other men had gathered around and were listening to his father. He felt proud.

"We had to learn," Oliver said. "Cochise said we could and he was right. When the government made us leave our own land and come up here to this strange place we brought our herd with us. It was very small in those days. We still didn't know enough about raising cattle. And this new place wasn't as good for the cattle as our own land was. But we learned and we made mistakes and for a long while it seemed it wouldn't work and all the time the army kept watch over us with their fingers on their triggers. But then the people learned and their sons learned and now we know and we have what we have."

The men sitting in a circle in the firelight with the open night above them and the stars close and the smell of the burning wood nodded and listened. That must have been the way it always was in the night in the old days, Joe thought. He had never felt so proud of his father.

Twelve

Joe listened to the beating of the drums. He watched the masked dancers jumping up and down, giving forth their bird noises. He looked around. Most of the people watching were Apaches, but there were some white people. He felt ashamed for what they were seeing.

The white people must be laughing. The whole thing was barbaric. If he were not an Apache, if he were a white man, he knew he would be laughing at what he saw.

He had almost not believed it when his father had told him one of the Apache girls was going to have a coming-out party. There hadn't been one on the reservation for a long time. The origin of the puberty rite went back to White-Painted-Lady and to Child-of-the-Water. Those were the deities the Apaches used to believe in in the old days. He didn't know anybody who believed in White-Painted-Lady and Child-of-the-Water today and yet here was the stupid ceremony being performed just as it had been, in the days when the whites called Apaches "gut-eaters."

When he was a child his mother had told him the old, almost forgotten legend. There were three deities. The chief god was called Usen, who was known as The Everywhere Spirit, who dwelt in the sky and who was invisible. That much Joe could believe, even now. He believed in a Being up there.

But then there was the mother goddess, White-Painted-Lady. White-Painted-Lady was supposed to have stretched out in the forest and the rain fell upon her and that was how her son was born and that was why he was called Child-of-

64

the-Water. Joe knew the Christians believed in a Mother with a Son born immaculately, and if they wanted to believe that, that was their business. He couldn't.

He remembered a story his father had once told him about Child-of-the-Water. When Child-of-the-Water was born the people had to live under the earth. They were forced to stay there by a giant. Child-of-the-Water was given the task to kill the giant so the people could come out into the sun. Child-of-the-Water tried everything but failed until a little bird lit on his shoulder and whispered to Child-of-the-Water to hit the giant in the heel. Child-of-the-Water made a sling and put a stone in it and hit the giant in the heel and the giant fell over dead. The people were freed from their imprisonment.

Joe was only a boy when his father had told him that story and at first he had thought his father had made it up to entertain him. Later when he found that in the old days the people had believed it had happened that way, he was embarrassed for them.

He was filled with shame for what he was seeing now. The white missionaries had researched it the way they would the early religious beliefs of any primitive tribe. Joe didn't like the idea of being a member of a primitive tribe.

The legend was that White-Painted-Lady herself had directed that certain rituals be performed when a young girl entered womanhood. That was to give her a good life. Back in the beginning, when White-Painted-Lady was still on earth, the first child who had the ceremony was identified with the goddess and was referred to by the name of the goddess and for the length of the ceremony was considered to be the symbol of the goddess.

The costume that first child wore was copied from the clothing White-Painted-Lady wore and the ceremony was arranged by the goddess, and that was the way it was conducted from that time on.

65

The ceremony had been held often in the old days. It was almost never held now. It lasted for four days and it was a big expense for the father of the girl. He had to provide food and drink for everybody for the entire four days. More than that, perhaps, was the attitude of the young Apache girls themselves. Most of them thought these old ceremonies were silly. Few of them could imagine themselves as a goddess, even for four days.

Joe had gone to the place where the rite was being held early in the evening. Some of the men he worked with on the range were going to attend and they had asked him to join them. He didn't feel good about going and when he got there and saw the white people standing around he felt even worse.

He saw the wickiup where the girl had to remain for the four days. He saw Apaches going in and out of the wickiup, which had been erected for this special occasion under the supervision of a shaman and which was considered sacred. Some of the women carried small children. During the ceremony the girl was supposed to have the power of White-Painted-Lady and people came to her to be blessed and to be cured of ailments. They brought babies for the girl to touch and promise a good life.

Joe heard someone talking. It was the missionary who had visited him in jail. The little man was giving a lecture about the ceremony to the white people.

"The girl has been given instructions by an old lady, probably an aunt. She has been told that whatever she thinks or does during these four days will determine the course of her life," the missionary said.

His tone sounded familiar, what he was saying and the way he was saying it. It was the voice of the professional lecturer. Joe tried to remember where he had heard it before.

"She must eat well, so she will always have plenty to eat," the missionary went on. "She mustn't talk too much because

66

then she will become a gossip." The missionary looked slyly at his white listeners. "A type of woman as much disliked by Apaches as by civilized peoples."

The white people laughed. Even that laughter was familiar to Joe. It had all happened before.

"She must not wash until the ceremony is ended," the missionary continued. "Because she would then bring about rain and spoil the people's fun. She must not get angry or use bad language because then she will always be that way. She must speak the truth because if she does not a curse will strike the tribe. And finally she must listen to everything the shaman sings in his songs and she must believe him because if she does not nothing he says will benefit the people."

The missionary paused. The white people nodded. Joe noticed that many of them were strangers. They were not from the Bureau. They were ranchers and townspeople from the outside. They must have been invited to the spectacle by the Agent or the missionary or somebody.

"At one time the Apaches believed all of this," the missionary said. "Few of them do now."

It came to Joe suddenly, the voice, the manner, the superior attitude. The missionary sounded just like the army instructors telling troops about the quaint customs of the simpleminded Vietnamese. He had listened to lectures like that many times, addressed to him as a civilized man from a civilized country.

"What do they believe in now?" a woman asked.

"Not Christianity, I'm afraid," the missionary said sadly. "We have largely failed to teach them the truth. But we continue to try."

Joe felt the anger rise in him and he wanted to make some answer and he wanted to run away. He did neither.

He watched the dancers and he had to admit that maybe the missionary had a point. The dancers were supposed to represent good spirits and evil spirits and they were capering around, screeching. He knew that some of those dancers had been men he had worked with on the range. How could they be so silly now?

"When the sun started to set the dancers went off onto a hill where a special brush shelter had been created for them," the missionary said. "There they were stripped and then they put on ritual shirts and moccasins. The shaman rolled a leaf of tobacco and puffed smoke to the four directions and asked that the dancers face east."

The missionary opened a small notebook and took a pencil flashlight from his shirt pocket. "This is what the shaman chants to the men," he said. He read from the notepad:

" 'The great Black Mountain Spirit resides inside the Big Star Mountain. He can be seen to the east under the heavens. The design of his body is fixed and unchanging and the big stars have created the uprights of his headdress. The Mountain Spirit rattles his headdress as he dances around the fire and drives away diseases. He sends away all evil and brings good.' "

The missionary closed the notebook and flicked off the flashlight.

"How wonderfully weird," a white woman said.

The white people who listened to the missionary could see Joe standing there but it made no difference to them. It was as though he was not there, or as though he could not understand the English language.

"After that the dancers start to paint their bodies," the missionary went on. He opened the notebook and turned the flashlight on it again. "I have made extensive research into this," he said, "and this is what the shaman sings at this point."

> The Holy Mountain,
> The Holy Mountain,
> There it is. And

In its middle, in its body
There stands a brush-built hut.
This brush-built hut is for the Mountain Spirit.
This is what he says.
This is what the Mountain Spirit in his brush-built
       hut in the Holy Mountain says:
In these moccasins flash Lightning,
I am Lightning, flashing and blazing,
There is life here, in this headdress,
In the noise of its pendants there is life,
The noise is heard and it sounds and my song
       is around these dancers
And protects them.

The missionary turned off the flashlight. One of the women shivered.

"It's scary," she said.

"You are perfectly safe here," the missionary said.

"Not like the old days," one of the white men said.

The missionary went on to say that when the shaman finished singing the dancers ate special food prepared for them and then they put on their masks. These were soft pliable helmets with drawstrings around the necks and two slits cut for eyeholes. The hoods were painted in all colors. Built into them on top were strips of slats, pointing up vertically and at angles and bound together across their tops by other slats, the superstructure rising more than a foot above the dancers' heads. Hanging from the ends of the slats were loose pieces of wood which rattled as the dancers moved.

"That was the design created in the ancient days and they are followed exactly to this day," the missionary said.

"They're cute," one of the white women said. "I'd sure like to have one of them to decorate my den."

The missionary shook his head. "Impossible. The people consider those masks so holy that right after the ceremony they are destroyed, and in a special, prescribed way."

69

"Sure you can't buy one for the little woman?" a man asked.

"I'm afraid not."

"Money talks."

"I'm sorry," the missionary said firmly.

Now the dancers were jumping and chirping louder than ever. They danced around the fire, throwing their arms about, jumping, rattling their headdresses, and the drums kept beating and the shaman was chanting. The dancers jumped to great heights that seemed even greater in the twisting flames. The Apaches who watched them shrieked in fear because that was what they were supposed to do; they were, as watchers, part of the act. The white people near Joe stared in fascination. The woman who had wanted a headdress for a souvenir gaped, her mouth opened slightly. As the dancing got wilder and wilder and the Apache audience shrieked louder she moved closer to her husband who put a protective arm around her.

"Makes you kind of wonder," the husband said.

"Oh, this is a rare opportunity to see a genuine native ceremony," the missionary said with enthusiasm.

Joe went away. The white people didn't seem to notice his leaving any more than they had noticed his being there. He went to join his friends from the range, who were sitting around drinking tiswin. He had several drinks of the beer, which was brewed stronger now than it was in the old days. It was almost as strong as the Australian beer they had in Nam. It wasn't very cold and that made it seem even stronger.

He saw Jennie Gates. She tried to approach him inconspicuously. There was an expression of concern on her face. What was she worried about, he wondered? He wasn't doing anything any of the other men weren't doing. He was drinking beer and watching the show same as they were.

He turned away from her to watch the dancers again. They were worshipping the fire from the four directions. They were supposed to be blowing away evil spirits and sickness. Joe wondered whether the missionary was explaining that to his listeners. From one side of the fire there was a steady beating of drums and a rattling of gourds. The shaman started to sing. His voice was low but it penetrated. Joe listened to him. Then Jennie tugged at his arm and asked if she could get him something to eat. Joe shook his head. He was beginning to feel good from the beer and he didn't want to lose that.

The shaman told of the beliefs of the people and of the things they feared and held holy. He sang in Apache and Joe was pleased with himself that he understood a little of what the shaman was saying. His parents had made him learn the Apache language and he had not forgotten it altogether. Many people his age couldn't speak it at all.

The shaman sang of the girl in the wickiup and he told of her childhood. He sang of the sweetness of girlhood. It was like the opening of flowers under the sun. He led her through gardens of flowers and through all the seasons. He told of the full cycle that was given to her, from the sprinkling of pollen to the final fulfillment of nuts and fruits.

A bottle was put into Joe's hand. He looked down at it. It was a bottle of whiskey. He lifted the bottle and drank some of the whiskey. He saw Jennie looking at him more worried than ever. Because of that he had another swallow of the whiskey. It burned his throat but it tasted good.

He listened to the shaman. The shaman sang:

> To White-Painted-Lady I have come,
> To her blessing I have come,
> To her good fortune I have come,
> To her long life and the grace of her
>   days I have come.

71

This is the song of her long life,
This is the song of her life in the sun,
With this holy truth I have come to her.

Joe had another drink of whiskey. He wondered what the white people were thinking about all this by now.

Suddenly the bottle was taken away from him by a man. It was one of the men who had agreed to go into business with him and who had backed out after the trial and the sentence.

Joe went to a food table and poured some tiswin into a paper cup. Jennie was at his side. She asked him not to drink anymore. He emptied the paper cup.

"Don't follow me around," he said. He wasn't sore at her. He just didn't want her to follow him around.

All this time the masked dancers were leaping around and the people were echoing the shaman the way people in a church might chorus the preacher and the drums kept up beating and the gourds rattled and the shaman seemed to weave in the flames blown around by the breeze. Even the wickiup seemed to sway.

Somebody stuck another bottle of whiskey into Joe's hand. He drank deeply.

"Please, Joe," Jennie said.

"This man is my friend," Joe said reasonably. "I can't insult him, can I?" He had another drink and the bottle was taken away.

The drums never stopped. He felt like they were banging inside his head. He kept thinking about the Agent and how the Agent had put him out of business.

He couldn't listen to the drums anymore. His head was splitting. And all of it was getting in the way of his thinking about the Agent. He had to get away from the noise so he could think a little better. He had lots of things to think about. He drank some more beer to clear his head but it did not clear his head.

By now he didn't care about the way Jennie was watching him. The hell with her. He didn't care about anything except to get away somewhere where he could be alone and think about the Agent and what the Agent had done to him.

He walked away. He knew he wasn't walking exactly straight. He didn't care about that either. He had to get away from the drums and the crazy dancers and from Jennie.

He heard Jennie ask him where he was going. He didn't answer. He waved her away. She didn't go away. She asked him again. She kept asking him and he did not answer and finally she stopped asking and after a while she stopped trying to keep up with him.

And that was good. He was alone.

Thirteen

Bill Hunter opened his eyes and heard the tapping on the door. He had the feeling he had been hearing it in his sleep for some time.

"Who can that be?" Winnie asked. "What time is it?"

Hunter looked at his watch. It was almost midnight. Earlier he and his wife had watched the masked dancers for a while and then had come home and had gone to bed. That was more than an hour ago.

The tapping continued. It was gentle, almost apologetic.

Winnie was half raised on her elbow. She watched as Hunter put on his bathrobe. He hurried to the door and the tapping continued. It was delicate but insistent. He opened the door. It was Jennie Gates and she was scared stiff.

"Jennie, what's the matter?" he asked.

"Please come help, Mr. Hunter," she said.

"Joe?"

"He's drunk. He's on his way to Mr. Lawton's house."

"Good Lord! I'll be right with you."

Hunter told his wife, dressed fast and rushed out. As they hurried along toward where the Agent lived Jennie told him what had happened.

"I tried to stop him from drinking so much," Jennie said. "He wouldn't listen to me. He said it would be an insult to his friends. They kept calling him a war hero and said he had to have a drink with them."

"What the devil is he going to see the Agent about at this hour?"

"The young men called him a famous warrior and said he had to drink with them," she said.

74

"What has the Agent got to do with all that?" Hunter asked.

"He said something about the Agent putting him out of business."

"Good Lord," Hunter said again.

They were not far from the Agent's house by then and Hunter looked around but he couldn't see anybody. There was almost a full moon and the stars were bright the way they are on the desert in the summer. He turned around and headed for the great bonfire where the party was still in full swing. Then he caught sight of a shadow lurching along and he broke away from Jennie and caught up with it. The shadow was Joe Murdock all right and he was heading for the Agent's house.

Hunter grabbed Joe's arm. "Where the hell do you think you're going?"

Joe kept walking as though Hunter hadn't said or done anything. Trying to hold him back was like trying to stop a mustang. Even in the dark he could see Joe's face was set and his eyes were glazed.

"Joe, for God's sake, stop!" Hunter felt he could have been talking to a stone wall. "Joe, what do you think you're going to do?"

Joe didn't answer.

Hunter jerked his arm. "Joe, for Pete's sake, you'll get busted for real this time. You could spend years in the state pen for this."

There was no response. Joe marched along, a machine, dragging Hunter with him.

Hunter gave his arm another pull with all the strength he had. "Joe, you're acting like a fool! Let's get away from here before Lawton hears something."

Joe waved his arm and sent Hunter sprawling. He kept walking toward the Agent's big house.

Hunter picked himself up and ran after him. He caught up just as Joe had reached the Agent's door and was raising a fist to pound on it. Hunter tackled him. It was a long time since he had played football in school but he hadn't completely forgotten it and he brought Joe down.

Joe went over like a felled log. No part of him bent. He went down stiff.

"I want to see if he'll shake my hand," Joe said.

"Shut up."

"He said I never paid him a visit," Joe said.

"Shut up."

"I know he won't shake my hand. Then I'll take his arm and break it."

"For God's sake, shut up."

"Then I'll ask him why he had to put me out of business."

Joe said all this in a reasonable voice, making good sense to himself. He started to get up, pushing Hunter aside. Hunter heard some voices up above and he hauled back and hit Joe on the jaw as hard as he could. He heard Joe's head snap back and then fall to one side and he pushed him against the building behind the hedge. He heard the window above being opened. He clapped a hand over Joe's mouth.

"Who's down there?"

Hunter twisted his head and looked up and saw the Agent leaning out of the window.

Joe began to squirm. Hunter squeezed hard on his mouth. He felt as though his fingers would make holes in Joe's cheek.

"Is there anybody down there?" the Agent asked.

Hunter heard Mrs. Lawton call out from inside the house. "What is it, Townsend?"

"I could have sworn I heard someone down there," Lawton said. "Probably just some noise drifting over from that savage demonstration."

Joe again tried to free himself and Hunter tried to tighten

76

his grip and then the window was shut. After a moment Hunter let go of Joe's face. His hand felt numb. His fingers wouldn't straighten.

Joe rubbed his jaw. After a while he stood up. He didn't say anything. Hunter got to his feet. Joe looked at the front door. Hunter braced himself. He thought he was going to have trouble again and this time maybe he wouldn't be able to get off a punch that would do any good. Joe might even take a swing at him.

Joe walked away. Hunter followed him cautiously. He didn't know what Joe might have in mind. But Joe just walked back toward the party. Hunter stayed with him.

Joe kept walking toward the firelight. Hunter looked around. He didn't see Jennie anywhere. She must have got scared Joe would be sore at her for getting him into the act.

They crossed the parade ground. There were street lights on the parade ground and Hunter looked closer at Joe. He saw Joe's mood had changed and it wasn't for the better. There was such hatred in the lean face it almost took Hunter's breath away.

They were halfway across the parade ground when Joe stopped suddenly. They could see the party not too far from where they were standing. The masked dancers had finished and the people were having their social dance, men and women, arms folded, facing each other, dancing toward each other in a line and then dancing away. Off to one side of the two lines of dancers was the wickiup with the young girl inside. It was lighted by candles and people were still passing through.

"Look at them," Joe said. "No wonder everybody laughs at us."

"Who's laughing?" Hunter asked.

"I hope you're appreciating all this, Mr. Hunter," Joe said.

Hunter didn't say anything.

"I hope you know this is a rare opportunity to see a genuine native ceremony," Joe said.

Hunter thought it didn't look much different now than square dancing but he didn't say it. That would sound too pat. And he wanted Joe to do the talking.

"Going in there and having that little snot-nose bless them," Joe said. "Bless them!" he laughed derisively.

"Any religion is faith," Hunter said, knowing it sounded corny but believing it. "If they believe in it hard enough it might work."

"Bull!" Joe spat on the ground. "They're just what that missionary said. They're primitives. What kind of nonsense is that? White-Painted-Lady! Child-of-the-Water! Are you ready for that, Mr. Hunter?"

He turned his head and looked back at the Agent's house, standing by itself in the Indian Bureau residential section around the parade ground. Hunter could see the anger and the shame coming together.

Joe looked back at the dancing. "What did he call it? A savage demonstration."

"Joe," Hunter said.

"He was right," Joe said. "He was absolutely right. He was right in busting up my business. How can a savage be trusted to run a business?"

"Joe," Hunter said.

There was a shout of laughter from the dancers and Joe said, "That dirty rotten . . ." He pushed Hunter aside and started back for the Agent's house.

Hunter ran after him, grabbed him and steered him to his own house. He kept praying Joe wouldn't fling him to one side and go where he wanted to go.

But Joe let Hunter lead him. He seemed now to have passed into a rage that was blind and aimless and hopeless. It was as though he didn't know what was happening to him and he didn't much care.

78

At one point it seemed Joe remembered where he had wanted to go and he started to pull toward Lawton's house but Hunter held on and got him away. He got him finally to his house and into his car. Hunter got behind the wheel fast and started the motor.

He saw Winnie come to the window and he waved to her to signal all was okay.

Joe slumped in the front seat and stared through the windshield. Hunter could see his hands slowly opening and closing. He thought of Lawton and of Lawton's arm and of Lawton's neck.

He breathed a sigh of relief when they were outside the reservation gate.

Fourteen

Once on the state highway Hunter just drove. He had no destination, no goal, no plan. All he knew was that he wanted to cool Joe Murdock.

It was a white night. The hills were like pieces in a collage. The light-colored alkali earth reflected the pale light of the moon.

Joe stayed low in his seat. He didn't ask any questions. He didn't seem interested in where they were going.

Hunter glanced at Joe's hands a couple of times. They were resting easily now. The anger seemed gone out of them. He looked at Joe's face. It was bleak and tight.

"Tell me how it was," Hunter said after they had been driving for about fifteen minutes.

"How it was where? In the hoosegow? It wasn't bad."

"I didn't mean there. I meant in Viet Nam."

"Oh, there. Nothing to tell about that."

After a while Joe laughed. It wasn't a fun laugh.

"It was a gas, the army," Joe said. "Sometimes the guys would ask me how it was living on a reservation. They didn't know anything, nothing at all, about how things operate at a place like this."

"What did you tell them?"

Joe gave that laugh again. "I tried to build it up. Funny?"

Hunter didn't answer.

"I told them we ran our own show. I wanted to be proud of it."

Joe was silent again. The only sound was the tires on the highway. The mountain peaks pushed into the sky. They had dimension. They didn't lie flat. Hunter felt he could almost see behind them.

"Gut-eater," Joe said.

Hunter glanced at him.

"They tell me Lawton still calls us that."

Hunter didn't say anything.

"Everybody has such stupid ideas about Indians," Joe said. He shifted in his seat. He kept his eyes straight ahead. "Like they think Indians can't hold booze. Right? Like it has to do with the simple fact that it's because he's an Indian. Firewater. The way the West was won. Right?"

When Hunter still kept silent Joe turned to him. "Okay, Mr. Hunter, so I got a little stoned. But I drank enough to get a little stoned, the way anybody who drinks enough gets a little stoned. Haven't you ever drunk enough so you were a little stoned, Mr. Hunter?"

"It's been known to happen."

"But you don't want to break anybody's arm. That's what you're thinking. Right?"

"When I was in Korea there was one time I wanted to break somebody's head."

"Yeah?"

"A corporal. I was only a PFC. He was stomping over me all the time."

"Did you?"

"No."

"Somebody stop you? A pal? Maybe with a jeep to take you for a ride to cool you? Or did you have enough of that fine white man's control?"

"Somebody put my head in a pail of water. Like to have drowned me."

Joe laughed outright. Hunter felt better.

"People keep saying Indians have a special weakness for alcohol. Like it's in the blood. Goes a long way back. Pour enough firewater into an Indian and he'll go on the warpath. Remember Ira Hayes?" Joe asked.

"One of the men who raised the flag at Iwo Jima? I sure do. He died."

"Yeah. Froze to death on the desert near Phoenix. He was on his way home at night and he fell down drunk and froze. Everybody said, 'Poor Ira Hayes. Great hero but he turned out to be a drunk. Goes to show you. Indians can't handle the stuff.' Bull! You know why he drank so much? Sure, he was an Indian and he drank too much, but do you know why?"

"No."

"Because he was an Indian."

Hunter twisted his head. "But you just said—"

"He drank a lot because he was an Indian," Joe said vehemently. "But not for the reason you think. It was politeness, Mr. Hunter. Are you ready for that?"

Hunter looked at him again. There was a harsh look on Joe's face.

"Ira Hayes was a celebrity," Joe said. "Every time somebody saw him on the street in Phoenix they'd want to shake his hand and then they'd want to buy him a drink because that's the way the white man shows friendship, always the big handshake and then the drink. And where a white man in Ira Hayes' position would say no every once in a while, no thanks, I'll take a rain check, something like that, Ira Hayes couldn't do that. Because he was an Indian and the way Indians think, the dumb, stupid way Indians think, that would be an insult. That would be acting rude to someone who offered friendship. He was too polite to say no and in the end all that friendliness and all that politeness killed him. But only another Indian can understand that."

"Is that why you loaded on the booze tonight?"

"That's my business, Mr. Hunter."

82

"Over in Viet Nam when they asked about Indians did you tell them about Ira Hayes?"

Joe made that derisive sound again. "They wouldn't buy. Even when we were sitting around some bar and I was drinking drink after drink along with the rest of them."

Hunter took out his cigarettes and offered the pack to Joe. Joe shook his head.

"Gut-eaters," Joe said again. "Well, with what went on tonight I suppose he's got to be right."

Hunter still hadn't any idea where he was headed. He had thought he would drive around for a while and then go back to San Pedro. But he saw a crossroad approaching. Something nibbled in his mind. He remembered what it was and turned into the crossroad.

"What do you know about Cochise?" Hunter asked.

"Everybody seems to be asking me that."

"What do you know?"

Joe looked at him. "What the hell brought that up? Little White-Painted-Lady in her magic wickiup?"

"I'm asking you."

"I know he beat the cavalry and then he was screwed by the government just like all the other Indians have been screwed by the government."

"And that's it?"

"Sure there's plenty more, but what difference did it make?"

"He was straight. You could put it that way."

"And what good did that do him?"

"He kept his word. He never lied."

"And look what it got him—and all the rest of us."

"His mistake, if you can call it that, was in believing other people were as straight as he was. There have been other people in the world like that. Some of them have been called saints."

Joe guffawed. "Come off it, man. You trying to tell me Cochise was some kind of a saint?"

"No way," Hunter said. "I'm only saying I don't think he was a fool. He was too damned honest and that trapped him. I think he believed other people had principle too. Maybe that was being naive but I wouldn't call it stupid."

"Why all this about Cochise?"

"He was a fighting man."

"The best. No argument. So what?"

"When it was time to fight. When that time passed he adjusted."

"There's that word again." Joe looked out the window but he still didn't seem interested in where they were or where they were going. "Adjusted."

"He couldn't know he'd be betrayed. But that isn't the point. The point is that he realized that things could not stand still, that things have to change."

It was about then that Hunter saw ahead what he had been looking for. He drove another half a mile or so and then pulled the car over to the side of the road.

"Let's get out for a minute," Hunter said.

They got out of the car and stretched their legs. The night was brighter than ever. The moon was almost directly overhead. There was a clean, desert smell to the air.

Hunter pointed. "Know what that is?"

Joe looked. He frowned. Then he nodded his head.

"Ever see it before?" Hunter asked.

"No."

What they were looking at was a mountain range not far away and the formation of one part of the summit looked like a human profile.

"They tell me that in the old days the Chiricahuas called this whole place the Spiritland of Cochise," Hunter said. Without his being able to explain why, his voice came out low, as though he believed he was truly talking about something sacred. "They tell me those people believed that profile was the profile of Cochise. They tell me that after Cochise's death and for a long time afterward the Chiricahuas used to go there, like a religious pilgrimage."

Joe didn't make any reply and Hunter stared at the profile. He had passed it often but always during the day and he had thought it looked like a flat rock escarpment and that it required a substantial amount of imagination to see it as the side of a human face. But now in the night the profile had dimension and it was real. It had a shadow on the cheek and that dark spot seemed to make the eye socket alive.

He turned to Joe. The young Apache was looking at the formation. His mouth was pulled down in a tight line. Hunter couldn't make out what he was thinking to make his face go that way. He couldn't tell whether it was good or bad.

Then Joe suddenly threw back his head. He burst into laughter. He looked away from the profile to Hunter. He kept laughing. He looked like he wanted to hold his belly and roll on the ground.

Joe laughed for a long time. Each time he slowed down he started in again. He finally got himself in hand. He pointed to the profile and tried to say something. He went into another spasm.

Finally he said, "So that's what you were up to, bringing me here." He started laughing again. He jerked his thumb toward the rock formation. "What did you think that would do for me?"

Hunter couldn't come up with an answer to that. Nothing that would do any work just then.

"Mr. Hunter?" Joe asked again.

Hunter shrugged. He didn't know. He didn't know for himself why he had brought Joe there. He didn't know what he had hoped for.

Still laughing, shaking his head, Joe climbed back into the car. Hunter got behind the wheel. They went back to the reservation.

Fifteen

The time came round for Lawton's summer vacation. He called a final conference with his Deputy, who would be in charge of San Pedro while he was gone.

They went over a number of routine matters. Hunter wondered whether the Agent had any inkling about the attempt Joe Murdock had made to get to see him on the night of the puberty ceremony. Lawton made no mention of it but that didn't mean anything. Lawton had never referred to Joe Murdock's questioning of his motives during the trial either. And Hunter knew his boss knew all about that.

After finishing with the normal Agency affairs, including new bulletins from the Bureau in Washington, the possibility of a visit by a Congressional committee and other matters, Lawton told Hunter something else was pending, something out of the ordinary. A film company wanted to make a picture about the Apache wars and wanted to make it in Arizona, using real Apaches from the San Pedro Reservation instead of the usual Hollywood Indians.

Lawton picked up a letter with the studio's name printed on top. "They have asked for permission to send someone here to discuss the matter. I agreed to that. Now this is something that must be decided by the Council. We take no official stand one way or the other. My suggestion is that when this man arrives you arrange to take him before the Council and let him speak for himself."

After the business talk was over Lawton relaxed. He was always cheery before his holiday. He wished Hunter well and left.

Hunter made himself comfortable in the Agent's office. He sat in the big chair. It felt fine, even though Lawton's secretary sniffed audibly when she saw him there.

Three days later the studio emissary showed up. He drove onto the reservation in a red foreign convertible with an Italian marque. Before he had turned off the engine a crowd of Apaches had gathered around the car.

Watching from the window, Hunter saw the man, a plump little figure in his middle thirties with a head of long hair, wearing a flowery shirt with an open collar, get out of the car. The man looked at the Apaches and seemed to be wondering whether it was safe to leave his car. He finally decided he had no choice and went into the administration building.

Brought into the Agent's office he seemed a little disappointed not to be dealing with the number one man but he recovered. He introduced himself as Kevin Wayne and plunged enthusiastically into the project.

"The Apaches are really going to get a break in this one," he said. He wandered casually over to the window to take a look at his car. "A beautiful story, a really beautiful story. We have a gorgeous script, written by one of the finest talents in Hollywood. I tell you, the Apaches will love this."

He was prepared to go on when Hunter stopped him. "I'd like to listen to everything you have to say, Mr. Wayne, but you're only going to have to repeat yourself."

Wayne looked puzzled. "Repeat myself? To who?"

"The Tribal Council."

"What's that?"

"Just what it sounds like. They represent the tribe and decide on all tribal matters."

Wayne glanced out the window and then turned to Hunter. "You mean I got to sell the idea to Indians?"

"You could walk around the reservation and speak to anybody you liked. No law against that. You could round up your people one by one."

"Can't you just okay it? Why do I have to talk to anybody but you?"

"I just explained why." Hunter smiled. He knew what Wayne was thinking. He knew Wayne was thinking that if the Agent had been there instead of his Deputy the Agent would have saved him all this trouble. "It's all to your advantage, Mr. Wayne. Somebody's got to organize this within the tribe and the only body that can do it is the Council."

Wayne nodded. He looked unhappy.

The sunlight poured into the Council chamber. On one of the walls was a blowup of the Tribal Charter, the document that created the Council and specified how its members were to be elected from the different districts on the reservation. Listed on the Charter were the Indians' rights and their responsibilities.

The councilmen were gathered around a long table. There were twelve of them, plus Nahilzay, who sat apart from the others, gripping his war staff with its three eagle feathers.

The councilmen were responsible, sober-looking men, dressed for the occasion. Wayne, presented to them by Hunter, passed his eyes over the grave, expressionless faces. His gaze stopped at Nahilzay. Nahilzay had a face with a thousand lines, sharp as the edge of a hatchet, with eyes that seemed to have witnessed everything since the creation of time. He held the war staff thrust before him, and Wayne looked at the markings on it, at the jagged streaks symbolizing lightning, at the streaks of paint, at the notches. The man from Hollywood wondered what those notches signified.

Hunter nodded to Willis Chambers, one of the councilmen. Hunter and Chambers were friends. Hunter was a little sorry for Chambers because he could have been an even bigger man in his tribe if it were not for his wife. His wife was a Cherokee Indian who looked down on Apaches. She believed Cherokee Indians were more highly cultured. She was one of those who referred to Apaches as "gut-eaters."

There was a famous story about Marian Chambers. When Willis was elected to the Council he invited some friends to a cookout to celebrate. There was a lot of beer drinking and Marian got loose in the mouth. She started on her favorite subject, the bigotry shown against Indians in the United States. She went on and on and most people didn't listen because they had heard it before.

A little later one of the other people there mentioned he had gone to the movies in the auditorium on the reservation the night before and that, as always, white people were at the head of the line waiting to get in.

"I know," Marian Chambers said. "And that little wop girl who works for the Bureau, she's always the first one."

The story got around. Everybody felt sorry for Willis Chambers but it didn't do him much good. The other Apaches felt it was a man's responsibility to keep his woman in a proper place.

"This gentleman is from Hollywood," Hunter said on this morning. "He will tell you why he is here. I ask you to listen to him and then decide what you want to do."

Wayne was still looking around the room at the faces as though he still didn't believe he was there. But when he started to speak he was clear and simple. He emphasized from the start the picture would be of benefit to the Apaches.

"It will be seen by millions of people all over the world. People will see that the history books have not always told the truth. People will see that the Apaches were not just bloodthirsty savages, that they had a culture of their own, that they had a family life and customs and traditions by which they lived."

Hunter looked at Willis Chambers. He suspected Willis would have liked to have his wife hear this.

"The wars between the army and the Apaches were fought for many reasons," Wayne went on. "Up to now it has always been the white man's reason that has been shown in books and in movies. In this picture the Apache side will be shown equally."

The Council listened with the usual Indian courtesy. It was impossible for Hunter to read on their faces whether Wayne was getting to them.

Wayne paused, waiting for something. Whatever it was he did not get it. The councilmen sat as though they had heard nothing and were content to wait forever to hear nothing else.

Wayne took a deep breath and continued. "In addition to all this there will be considerable financial benefits. Your people will be paid for their work, and they will be paid at the same scale paid to white people who work on location."

One or two of the councilmen, including Willis Chambers, were nodding now. Lester Matthews just looked thoughtful. Hunter guessed he was wondering how he could make some of the Hollywood money stick to his fingers.

Having nothing more to say, Wayne shut up. Some of the councilmen cleared their throats. Nobody seemed to want to make a first move one way or another. Finally Lester Matthews, who was chairman of the Council, asked Hunter what he thought about it. Hunter said that the Agent had instructed him to report official neutrality.

"Mr. Lawton didn't feel one way or the other about this?" Lester Matthews asked.

"No."

"He made no suggestions at all?"

"None."

Satisfied that nothing would be done that the Agent might disapprove of, Lester Matthews sat back and began to think some more.

"Well then," he said, "we will talk about this among ourselves and we will tell Mr. Wayne what we have decided."

The other councilmen nodded and there was some smiling and Wayne wiggled his hand in a friendly way. He looked at Hunter questioningly and Hunter nodded to him to assure him that all seemed to be going well. The councilmen were talking among themselves, pairs of heads leaning together.

Hunter beckoned to Wayne to leave the room with him when Nahilzay thumped his war staff on the floor.

The genial conversation stopped.

Without looking at anyone, staring at a blank wall, Nahilzay started to speak in Apache. He started in a low voice, very low. He held his war staff in two hands and he seemed to be seeing something with his black eyes that no one else could see.

The moment the old man opened his mouth the atmosphere in the room changed, a new note had been introduced. From the almost inaudible voice Nahilzay warmed up and then he shifted from the guttural everyday Apache speech into the Apache big speech, which involved hand gestures as well and which was used only on important occasions.

Nahilzay's dark eyes filled with black fire and he pounded his hands together in sign language. He let the war staff fall against his chest and he used his hands more and more violently.

Wayne was lost. He looked at Hunter for some kind of explanation. Hunter could give him none.

But the Council was a different Council now. The men were no longer friendly. One by one their faces seemed to turn to granite. They shifted angrily in their chairs as the caustic sounds poured from Nahilzay's lips and his ancient, wrinkled hands made thunder in the air. One by one the Council looked at Wayne with open hostility. Even Willis Chambers looked at Wayne as an enemy.

92

Wayne leaned toward Hunter. He ran his finger around his shirt collar. "What is this all about?"

"I don't know," Hunter said.

He had no idea what Nahilzay was saying or how long he spoke and gestured but it seemed a long time and the chamber on that blazing Arizona day began to feel like the inside of a deep-freeze. Nahilzay finally subsided and he again wrapped his thin fingers around his war staff. All the time he had spoken he had continued to look through the blank wall, seeing his own vision and nothing else.

For a while nobody said anything. The room was like a vacuum. A vacuum filled with old anger.

Hunter realized he had to say something in his official capacity. "Mr. Matthews, unfortunately I could not understand what Nahilzay said. May I ask what it was?"

The councilmen swung their eyes on the Acting Agent. Hunter knew it was crazy but he felt a wave of nervousness. These men, whom he thought he knew fairly well, suddenly were strangers.

Lester Matthews answered him, and for once Lester Matthews did not sound like an Apache politician. "What our sage Nahilzay has said is this: Nahilzay says that not long ago someone came from the outside and asked to have some of our young men. The man from the outside said the young men would make money and would benefit the tribe. Nahilzay says the tribe believed that and gathered together young men, the finest and bravest of them all, and that the young men went away with the man from the outside and the people never saw the young men again."

Listening to Nahilzay's story put into English made the councilmen tighter than ever.

Hunter was bewildered. "I have been here for more than two years. I have never heard of this event."

"It happened," Lester Matthews said. "When Nahilzay spoke of it I remembered it. It happened."

93

One of the councilmen said, "I remember it too."

Another said, "And I."

Others grunted.

"When was this?" Hunter asked.

"It was at the time of Geronimo," Lester Matthews said.

He said it in an ordinary manner, stating a fact. Wayne sagged. Hunter held his face tight and fought down whatever demand for nervous laughter rose in him.

"The time of Geronimo," Hunter said carefully. "That was almost a hundred years ago."

"Yes," Lester Matthews agreed. "As Nahilzay said, it happened."

The other faces were still set.

Now Hunter thought how amazing it was. The power Nahilzay had. Combined with the fact that tribal memories were part of the blood. That was a big thing, the luring away by the government of Geronimo's braves, and it was not strange for Nahilzay to refer to that time as "not too long ago."

"With the permission of the Council, I would like to speak," Hunter said.

Lester Matthews gave him the tightest of nods.

"I do not argue for Mr. Wayne." Hunter said. "I want only to point out that what Nahilzay spoke about took place a century ago and that Mr. Wayne's people are not the people who kidnapped your warriors."

Willis Chambers inclined his head. It seemed to Hunter he was the first to be coming out of the spell cast by the old words of the old man about old times.

"Another thing," Hunter said. "There have been men who have been called away from here since the time Nahilzay spoke of. Many have been called away for the wars this country has fought. And if these men were favored so they did not die in battle they were always returned to their people. The latest is Sgt. Joe Murdock, who was away for three

94

years and who returned with scars on his body and with medals for bravery."

Outside the building Wayne looked around. He felt he was coming back from a long way away. Then, reassured by what he saw, real buildings, people moving about normally and, most of all, his red convertible, surrounded as always by curious Apaches, he said to Hunter, "They were kidding, weren't they?"

"I don't think so," the Deputy Agent said.

Wayne jabbed him lightly with his elbow. "It was a put-on, wasn't it? The dude from California. That kind of thing?"

"No."

"You mean they were serious?"

"Yes," Hunter said. "I think so."

Wayne lit a cigar. "Geronimo," he said. "My God."

The Council did not come to a decision as the hours passed. By the end of the day the men were still deliberating. Wayne had dinner with Hunter and his wife, Winnie, and then the Hollywood representative was put up in one of the guest houses on the reservation.

It was about five o'clock in the morning when Hunter was wakened by his doorbell. He turned on the night light and looked at his watch. He put on a robe and went to the door. It was Willis Chambers.

"The Council has just voted," Willis Chambers said. "It approves the making of the film."

Hunter looked at his watch again.

"It was Nahilzay," Willis Chambers said. "Nahilzay speaks strong words. We had to make him understand."

"Does he understand?"

"He has warned us to be wary." Willis Chambers looked owlish in the early morning light. "Nahilzay says the white man always speaks with a forked tongue."

Hunter nodded. "I know. Well, if the news is important enough to get me up at this hour it's important enough to pass along to Mr. Wayne. Wait till I put on some clothes."

The two men went to the guest house. Hunter knocked on Wayne's door. After a few moments Wayne asked who it was. Hunter told him. Wayne opened the door and peeked out. He looked uneasy.

Hunter told him of the Council's decision.

Wayne became a happy man. He was so happy he was dressed and rolling off the reservation in his red convertible in less than twenty minutes.

Sixteen

About a week later Judge Mel Moore paid a visit to the Murdock home. He checked in advance to make certain both Oliver and Joe were in from the range.

The Judge was made welcome. Florence Murdock put fresh coffee on the stove. There was no bad feeling because Judge Moore had put Joe in jail. That was over with. It was not talked about.

After he had a cup of strong coffee, Judge Moore went to work on a cigar and Oliver Murdock filled his pipe. When he was comfortable and the cigar was lit the Judge told the Murdocks more about the Hollywood film.

Joe laughed. It was not a happy laugh. "Another picture about savages with paint on their faces."

Judge Moore pursed his lips. "It may be more than that."

"How can it be more than that?" Joe demanded.

His mother looked at him worriedly. She did not like to hear him talking to an important man in that tone of voice. She was relieved to see that Judge Moore was not angry.

"We have been promised the picture will show our side of things," Moore said.

"History," Joe said. "Ancient history. Who gives a damn about that?"

Oliver now looked at his son in reproof.

"It is to be a picture that will deal with the times of Cochise," Moore said.

"Cochise," Joe said. "That's all I hear about."

"You could hear worse. Many of the things we know we have learned from him."

"It doesn't seem we have learned much," Joe said. He poured himself another cup of coffee. "A picture about Cochise. And what will that prove? Do you think people will go home thinking, gee, that Indian chief was something, wasn't he? Those white men were bastards, weren't they? No way."

"Joe," Oliver said.

"What will they see?" Joe asked. "Lots of fools all painted up, trying to pretend they're brave warriors? And all the important parts played by actors from Hollywood who'll walk around saying 'How.' " He drank some of the coffee. His face got tight. "Why can't they make a picture about how Indians live today? About how we live here?" He put down the coffee cup and got up and walked back and forth. The others looked at him but they said nothing. "We have an agent who treats us as schoolchildren. We have to buy from a robber and nobody does anything about that. This is our own land and they make us think they're doing us a favor by letting us live on it. Why doesn't somebody make a picture about that?"

Oliver Murdock would have stopped him from going on but Judge Moore gestured with his hand.

"And we have a pretty good reservation, from what I've heard," Joe said. "One of the better ones, I understand. What about the others? What about those poor people on the Papago Reservation? They're starving. This country is feeding half the world and letting them starve. They live in a ghetto. It's so bad that if they were blacks they'd be rioting and burning down cities."

"How do you know about this?" Judge Moore asked in a mild voice.

Joe turned on him. "I've been away, remember? I've been away for three years. I've been to places where they have newspapers and magazines and you can read about what's going on. Not here. Here it's like nothing has changed for a hundred years."

98

"Go on," Judge Moore said.

"Why? About the Papagos? How they have to walk miles just to get water? Why don't they make a movie about that? About how the Grandfather in Washington watches over his redskinned children today."

"I don't know," Judge Moore said.

Joe made his derisive sound. "Well, I know. There wouldn't be any fights and scalpings and killings and war paint and actors in soldier uniforms yelling 'Charge!' " He gave that snorting sound again. "No bugles, Judge. No wagon attacks. No torturing. Just poverty and sickness and death. And no complaining. That doesn't add up to a movie when the poor suckers don't even complain, does it?"

"Perhaps not," Judge Moore said in the same mild voice.

Joe faced him squarely. He leaned forward on his toes. He looked lean and worn down hard from the days on the range. "Why don't Indians riot, Judge?" he asked. "Why do the Indians just take it? Is it because we're all run by old men who are Indian Uncle Toms?"

"Joe," Oliver Murdock said. "I won't have that kind of talk in this house."

Joe turned to him. "Why not, Pop? Don't you believe in free speech? They told us that was one of the things we were fighting for over in Nam."

"You will not be rude," Oliver said firmly.

"Rude!" Joe clenched his fists and shook his head and for a minute he wanted to hit something and then his throat choked up and he wanted to apologize to his father. He knew that if his father had had his strength he would be even more forceful. He knew that by the way he was talking he was only exposing his father's weakness.

"You have brought up many things, Joe," Judge Moore said.

"It doesn't matter," Joe said. He wanted to leave the room. He wanted to go away and be alone.

"It does matter," Judge Moore said. Listening to Joe he had let his cigar go out. He relit it.

"It doesn't matter at all," Joe said. They were all crippled, one way or another, and that's why they all lived in a big jail.

"Why don't Indians make riots?" Judge Moore asked, as though he were asking himself. "It is true. Of course there have been a few disturbances and protests here and there but as a general rule our people don't riot. Why not? Other people do. Blacks do. People from Puerto Rico do. I even heard on the radio that the Mexicans in California were protesting."

"Everybody," Joe said. "All God's children. And we Indians were supposed to be the wildest of them all. And the Apaches the worst of all Indians."

Oliver and Florence Murdock were not so worried now. They saw that the Judge did not seem to mind the way Joe spoke and that the Judge was talking to him as an equal.

"It's got to do with the nature of the beast," Judge Moore said. "Maybe Indian nature doesn't go that way."

Joe laughed again. "Come on, Judge. You know better than that. You've seen the movies. Who comes screaming over the hill? Who does the butchering? Who gallops around the wagon train killing little children? Those old devil Apaches. Who else?"

Judge Moore nodded. "In the old days we were wild. Nobody worse, as you say. Even the other Indians around here were afraid of us. And as for the whites . . ." He shook his head. "They used to say that during the time of Cochise you could walk from one end of Apache Pass to the other without having to touch the earth, that's how thick the pass was with the bones of white people killed by Cochise and his men. Yes, we could be violent. They say that after Cochise was betrayed by a white army lieutenant and some of his relatives were shot that he swore to kill ten white-eyes for every Indian

100

killed. And he kept his word. They say Cochise put back the development of Arizona for a quarter of a century."

"What development?" Joe asked. "Gas stations and saloons and auto junkyards?"

The Judge ignored that. "But you know something, Joe, before Cochise and his men went about this violence they always held a ceremony. They danced and prayed. Everybody says that proves how savage they were, jumping up and down to the tom-toms."

"Well, weren't they?"

"White men never did that," Judge Moore said.

"Then it's true," Joe said. "Like those damned fools the other day with that girl in the wickiup."

"White men never had to do that," Judge Moore repeated. "The Apache was working himself up to the point where he could go out and fight and maybe kill. He prayed for help. He had to tighten his mind. He had to build passion."

Joe looked at him and frowned.

"The white man never had to do that," Judge Moore said. "He was civilized. He was so civilized he could pull the trigger automatically every time he saw an Indian." He looked at Joe intently. "Why don't we Indians stage riots, you asked. Maybe it has to do with our nature. Maybe it has to do with dignity. Maybe pride. Indians have been able to survive anything, from hunger to the arrival of the white man. Maybe those Papagos are weathering all this as though it's just something temporary, as though it hasn't been going on for years. Maybe they're too proud to riot. Does that sound stupid to you?"

After a moment, Joe said, "Yes." He sat down. He thought he must have more answer than that but he couldn't find it.

Judge Moore said, "I've been selected by the Council to act as go-between with the movie people."

Oliver and Florence congratulated him. They were relieved to get off the other subject. Joe was uninterested.

"I have to round up people," Judge Moore said. "About two hundred and fifty for the start. Maybe more later."

"It's a big job," Oliver said gravely.

"Too much for one man," Judge Moore said. "I need an assistant. What about you, Joe?"

Joe looked up amazed.

"You know something about people," Judge Moore said.

"What makes you think that?"

"You didn't get stripes in the army for nothing."

Florence Murdock reached out and touched her husband's hand. It was not like her to do that in public.

"No way," Joe said.

"Joe," Oliver said. This time there was power in his voice.

"I'm sorry, Pop," Joe said. "It's just that the whole idea is crazy."

Judge Moore was lighting a fresh cigar. He raised his eyes. "People will earn money."

"So?"

"You said you were sorry for the other people, the Papagos."

"That's hitting below the belt, Judge."

"The better this picture goes the more money our people will make." The Judge stood up. "You will be in charge of getting the young men. You have been working with them on the range long enough to know them, more or less. Pick about thirty or forty good ones. Everybody will know they are from our tribe."

Joe started to say something but by then the Judge was making his farewells to the Murdocks.

Seventeen

"Why are you doing this?" Henry Sloane asked. "Why are you in charge of this?"

Henry Sloane was a powerfully built young man. He stood up with his arms folded across his chest. He was wearing levis and boots.

The other men gathered on the range looked at Joe for an answer. Joe had called them together to tell them that he was going to select some men for the picture. He hadn't expected any trouble. He was surprised when Henry Sloane challenged him.

He tried to think about what he knew about Henry Sloane. He remembered that Henry Sloane was a very good horseman and that a lot of the young people admired him.

"I didn't know the picture was going to be about jail," Henry Sloane said.

"It isn't," one of the other Apache youths said.

Henry Sloane made a wildly exaggerated gesture of surprise. "But if Joe Murdock has anything to do with it what else can it be about?" Henry Sloane nodded slowly. "That answers the question, why Joe was given this job."

Joe hadn't anticipated any of this. He felt he had been conned into the job by Judge Moore but then he set about to do it with twenty-twenty vision, based on standards and gauges he had learned in the army.

"Well," Henry Sloane said. "We don't want to be in a picture about a jail, do we?"

A couple of the other young men laughed. The others were waiting for Joe to say something.

"Okay, Henry, you're a funny man. Now let's get on. I need about thirty men," Joe said.

"You heard him," Henry Sloane said. "He learned to talk like that in the army. You heard him."

"Knock it off," Joe said.

"Wasn't that what the white agent said to you?" Henry Sloane asked. "And you obeyed."

"I said knock it off," Joe said.

"And you're still obeying white man's orders," Henry Sloane said. "That's why you're here, isn't it?"

Joe, squatting, jumped to his feet. Out of nowhere Henry Sloane had a knife in his hand and a fresh smile on his face and the other Apaches backed away and made a circle. It had been a long time since there had been a real fight.

Joe looked at the knife. There was nothing cowardly in Henry Sloane's pulling it. Joe had his own knife. All the men carried them. It was natural for Henry Sloane to pull his knife. He was astonished when Joe did not draw his.

Instead, Joe went into a crouch, his hands held in front of him, his arms half bent. He stalked Henry around inside the circle. He knew what he had to do. He had to put down Henry Sloane and he had to put him down all the way and he needed bare hands to do that.

The other men watched, grunting in their excitement. They thought Joe was crazy not to get out his own knife.

Henry Sloane was agile and he jumped around and kept up a running fire of remarks. Joe just followed Henry around, his hands open. Then Henry took a swipe with his knife. He kept talking and swung his arm suddenly. Joe dodged. Henry laughed and the men watching let out shouts of encouragement, mostly to Henry. Most of them still thought Joe was a fool to keep his knife sheathed.

Joe kept moving after Henry and Henry kept capering around making insults and then he took another swipe at Joe and at that moment Joe made his play.

104

The men watching said later they never saw anything move as fast as Joe's right hand. One moment Henry Sloane's knife was flashing in the sun and the next moment Joe had Henry's knife wrist in a grip. The other men talked a lot about it later. They all said none of them saw Joe's hand move.

And when Joe had the wrist in his grasp Henry Sloane stopped dead, not just the knife arm, all of him. It was, the men said when they talked about it afterward, as though Joe had found a secret nerve in Henry Sloane's wrist and had paralyzed him.

Joe held him that way a little while and then he tightened his hold and Henry Sloane's hand got slack and the knife fell to the ground. Joe reached out with his other hand and grabbed Henry Sloane's left wrist. All the time Henry Sloane didn't move. He stared at Joe as though he was hypnotized.

Then Joe lifted Henry Sloane off the ground. He lifted him by his arms. He held him dangling just above the ground for a moment or two and he lowered him slowly.

And all that time, the Apaches watching said many times later, Henry Sloane made no move of his own. He could have kicked Joe but he didn't.

After Joe set Henry Sloane back on his feet he bent down and picked up Henry's knife and handed it back to him, handle first.

Then Joe squatted again. He took out a little black pad from the back pocket of his levis. He took out a small yellow pencil and wet the tip.

"I'm putting you on the list of the men I'll need, Henry," Joe said. "I'm putting your name on the list first."

Eighteen

The seven Apache boys ran around and around in a great circle in the hot sun on the flinty ground. Their faces were screwed up tight to keep their mouths shut. Their fathers and other Apaches squatted on their haunches and watched.

One father said, "My boy is good."

Another father said, "My boy is better."

The first father said, "A horse."

The second father said, "Good."

Off to one side Cochise stood and watched, his arms folded across his chest. His face was proud as he saw how the boys kept their lips pressed together as they ran.

One boy stubbed his toe on a stone. He cried out in pain and water spilled from his mouth, down his chin and onto his chest. He stopped running. He walked off the course, his head hanging. His father, disgraced, got up and went away.

The boys reached the last lap. Their fathers and the other men shouted encouragement. Many bets had been made and the men were excited.

The boys crossed the finish line. One by one they opened their mouths and emptied them of the water they had held there during all of the race. They did this to prove they had not spat out the water secretly while on the far side of the course.

The father who lost paid off his bet of a horse. Others paid or collected bets they had made. The race was ended and everybody felt good, even the losers.

Cochise spoke to the boys. "You must do this many times. You must learn to jog in the sun and hold water in your mouth. It will give you good lungs and teach you to be a master of yourselves. You did good things today."

In another part of the Apache encampment a little later other boys were trained in the sport of throwing stones against each other. They faced each other across a distance of about twenty feet. They had to learn to dodge the stones or they could get hurt. Cochise watched them too. He told them it was good. It would teach them to be quick in battle.

In the middle of the rancheria women worked pounding deer brains into the hides of deer, making the skins soft and pliable, ready to be made into breechclouts and high moccasin-boots and jackets. Men sat on their haunches and carefully fixed obsidian points onto balanced sticks to make them into arrows. People went in and out of wickiups. Women stirred meat stews in pots over open fires. There was a smell of wood smoke.

Cochise saw everything and approved. He loved his people. It was his happiness when the hunt had been good and they had food to cook and skins to treat.

And everywhere the camera followed him, its single, all-seeing eye recording everything. The camera had a life of its own, Joe had come to feel, a life which belonged to it and which could not be disturbed or altered. The camera moved everywhere. It might have been a creature from another world, a space-age visitor inspecting life on an alien planet. The men who operated it had become in Joe's eyes nothing but subordinates, an entourage in attendance.

At the beginning Joe had felt himself a visitor from another place too and he had felt he belonged with the camera and he had seen the Apaches in their ancient dress as strangers. But as the days passed it had changed with him and he knew he was not looking at people from another world but at his own people as they had been. He was looking at himself. He was everywhere. He was running in

107

the water race with the children and he was dodging stones and he was making bows and arrows.

The studio research had been thorough. All was as it had once been in this re-creation of an old-time Apache village a few miles outside the reservation. The men and women and most of all the children had taken easily to the transformation. It was not a transformation, Joe had come to understand. The levis and the American shoes and the Mother Hubbards were transformations. This was a strange reality.

Even Cochise was reality. The man, a Hollywood actor as Joe had expected, had been a disappointment when Joe first had seen him. He was pleasant enough and he had close-cropped gray hair and he was sitting sprawled in a camp chair smoking a cigarette. Then he was called before the camera and Joe witnessed a miracle.

A woman fitted a long, black wig on his head and he stood up and in some magical way something happened. He became Cochise. It was something as simple and as inexplicable as that. And when he spoke he spoke as Cochise and when he spoke he was listened to, not only because that was the way it had to be for the picture, but because of what he gave from himself.

When Joe first had seen him he had wondered how he would feel. How he should feel. He was prepared to be scornful. When he first saw the actor his expectations were realized. But after the actor put on the wig and got before the camera Joe was confused. After a while it got so that when the actor was not before the camera, when he was not in his wig, that it was then he seemed unreal to Joe. It was as though Cochise was pretending to be a Hollywood actor.

Joe was considered by the film people to have done a tidy job. He had produced, in the end, some fifty young men to play the parts of warriors. He had chosen his men carefully. He had refused to play a part in the picture himself.

He heard his name called. It was the director, Orrin Wesley, a genial, suntanned man, who was now sitting under the shade of a tree, puffing on a pipe, as though he too were a visitor, as though he had nothing to do with the life and commotion all around.

"Yes, Mr. Wesley," Joe said.

"Those bloodthirsty warriors of yours, they're over in that clearing, getting a lesson in how to kill us poor white men. Have a look at them and see that everything is okay." The director always talked that way, kidding, but he never offended.

"Yes, sir," Joe said.

He walked through the forest. He knew what this was all about. It had been a funny thing, all around. It was something no one had anticipated.

He heard some orders being given and he hurried on and came to the clearing. He saw what he had expected to see and yet it was a strange sight. There were about forty or forty-five young Apaches, all in the old dress, and there was a fat little man in a flowered shirt and red slacks with sweat running down his face.

Joe went to the little fat man and asked him how it was going.

"Terrible," the little man said. He shook his head.

As Joe watched he went to one of the young Apaches who was holding a bow and arrow as though he had never before seen a bow and arrow, and which, until a couple of days before, he never had.

"No, no, no," the little fat man moaned. "Not that way, this way!"

He corrected the Apache's grip and the young man aimed the arrow at the target and let go. The arrow went almost straight up. The little fat man clapped his hand to his head and moaned again.

109

The Apache wandered over to Joe. Joe saw now that under the war paint he was Henry Sloane. Henry waggled his bow. He and Joe had become friends. Joe had made him his assistant.

"How does it go?" Joe asked.

"Lousy. Do you mean our ancestors really used these things?"

"Yes."

Henry Sloane shook his head. "I think they just invented them for the movies."

They watched a fierce-looking brave trying to fit his arrow to the bowstring. He jiggled it for a moment or two and then the arrow went off, almost hitting another Apache. Again the little fat man threw up his hands.

Joe remembered when Mr. Wesley had reported it to him. "Not one of them, Joe, not a blessed one of them ever shot a bow and arrow."

"That doesn't surprise me, Mr. Wesley," Joe had said. "Bows and arrows have not been Apache armament for some time."

"It's funny, for some reason. One of those men told me he could strip a machine gun blindfolded."

"That doesn't surprise me either. Some of them were in Korea."

"It still doesn't seem right. You see, Joe, I'm the biggest movie fan of them all. I believe movies. I believe those lads are real Apache warriors."

Joe had thought Mr. Wesley must be crazy until he had got to believe in Cochise himself, the actor Cochise.

Joe heard some laughter now and looked up and saw that the little fat man looked as though he was going to cry. The little fat man had come as a surprise. When he appeared, no one had known who he was. Then Wesley called all the young Apaches together and told them that the little fat man

110

was one of the world's champion archers. He came from Brooklyn, Wesley said, and he laughed because that seemed to tickle him.

"I have made many films," he said to the Apaches. "It's a weird business. But I have never before had to hire a man from Brooklyn to teach Apaches how to shoot arrows."

The Apaches had looked at the little fat man, whose name was Sam Robinson, a little skeptically. They thought the director was playing some kind of joke. Sam Robinson corrected that impression immediately. He took some arrows and a bow and put on a demonstration. He shot an arrow into a tree and then shot a second arrow which split the first one.

Joe watched a little more now. He saw one Apache almost put out his own eye. He saw another shoot an arrow straight into the ground, almost hitting his own foot.

Sam Robinson couldn't take it any longer. He had to let off some steam. He slung a quiver over his back and waved for the Apaches to give him room. He reached over his shoulder and whipped out an arrow from the quiver and fired it at the target. Before the arrow reached there he had another on its way. He kept that up, pulling out arrows, firing them with blinding speed, and all of them hit the target and some of them hit dead center.

When he was finished his shoulders sagged in exhaustion. The Apaches jumped around and cheered.

The bows and arrows weren't the only problems. The Apaches had difficulty riding horses. They could ride well but they were used to riding like everybody else, with saddles. The research department at the studio had determined the original Apaches didn't use saddles or stirrups. They rode bareback, or at most threw a blanket over their horses. The men today had never ridden bareback. They didn't know how.

At night, after the day's work, Joe thought about all these

things. It seemed to him that Apaches had no place to go now. In the world of the white man they were Indians. Now, trying to be Indians, they knew too much about the white man's ways to be truly Indians. They could slip into the parts but they couldn't do the real things. They were in the middle, neither one thing nor the other. They could pretend to belong to either world or both worlds but they belonged to neither.

A couple of nights later they were shooting the wedding scene between the white hero and his Indian sweetheart. Joe saw Bill Hunter and his wife. The Deputy Agent waved to him to join them. Joe went over and hunkered down next to them. He looked around. The encampment was real enough during the day but at night it was stunning. Fires were lit and people moved around and the pointed tips of the wickiups stabbed at the sky. The equipment vanished in the darkness. Even the camera, with its glassy, unblinking eye, was lost.

Hunter touched Joe's arm and pointed. Joe saw Jennie Gates in a buckskin costume. She wore a pendant and bracelets. Joe had not known she had been taken on for the wedding scene. He waved to her. He said hello. She had an air of gravity he had never seen before and when she answered her voice was different from the voice he was used to. She made him feel nervous. She had another life too, he thought. Maybe it was that she too had no life at all.

Jennie moved on and Joe got his first look at the shaman who was going to marry the lovers. His name was Owl Eye and he was imported from Hollywood. He was a magnificent-looking Indian with a big, round, impressive face.

Wesley called for silence. Then he called for action. The white man and the Indian girl, who actually was a white Hollywood actress, walked up to the shaman and knelt before him.

Owl Eye opened his mouth and spoke. The words came

112

out in a high-pitched tenor. The enunciation was almost pure Oxford English.

People laughed.

"Cut!" Wesley yelled.

Owl Eye looked around. He seemed bewildered.

Wesley got up and walked over to the actors. He spoke to the white hero. "Jimmy, you didn't walk up to Owl Eye in the right way. We'll try again."

The scene was started again. Owl Eye forgot his lines. Wesley called "Cut!" again. Puffing calmly on his pipe, he said, "Don't worry, Owl Eye, the lighting wasn't the way I wanted it anyway."

They tried again. Owl Eye got more and more rattled. He kept blowing his lines. Wesley never lost his composure. He always came up with a reason why the scene would have had to be redone anyway. Once he said the extras weren't grouped properly. Another time he said the Indian bride hadn't looked at the groom at the right time.

Joe tried to understand what was going on. He knew something was going on. He didn't know very much about making pictures but he could tell the director was making excuses. He didn't know why.

Hours passed. The scene had to be done over and over again. Each time between takes somebody had to go around and make sure the set was clean, that nobody had left a cigarette butt where the camera might pick it up. One time as Wesley was getting ready to roll somebody spotted a Coke bottle in a crotch of a tree that would have been right in the middle of the screen.

It was after one o'clock in the morning when they finally got the scene on film to print. The set broke up. Hunter took Joe back to the reservation.

"That damned fool!" Joe said. "Why couldn't he have learned his lines?"

113

"Beats me," Hunter said.

"Do you have any idea what that idiot cost the studio?"

"None."

"Thousands. Thousands. They had three more scenes scheduled to be shot tonight."

Hunter looked at Joe with interest. He hadn't known Joe had become so interested in studio expenses. "And it never mattered."

"What never mattered?" Joe demanded. "He had to say his lines, didn't he? Even in that squeaky voice."

"Wesley talked to me earlier. He told me Owl Eye had been sent on from Hollywood without a screen test. He said when he heard the Indian speak he knew he would have to dub in another voice for him back at the studio."

"I don't get it," Joe said.

"You can't have an Indian shaman sounding like an English butler."

"I get that. I wondered about that accent. But if they're going to use another voice why did Wesley keep doing it over and over again?"

"Owl Eye doesn't know they're going to give him a new voice."

Joe frowned.

"Neither does anyone else working in the picture."

Joe was silent. "All those excuses Mr. Wesley thought up, blaming everybody else."

"Yes," Hunter said.

"Are you trying to tell me they were trying to save that old man's face?"

"Does that surprise you, Joe?" Hunter asked.

Cochise stood erect, his head high, facing the men seated in a semicircle on the earth before him. The Chiricahua chief wore buckskin and there were bands of leather on his wrists.

114

A turquoise amulet hung from his neck. A leather band was bound around his forehead. His long black hair fluttered in the breeze.

"The white man comes here in increasing numbers," he said. His face was like iron and his voice was stern. "They are like grains of sand on the desert. They are like leaves on the trees. They are like ants. We slay them and we defeat them and they come more and more."

The squatting men grunted.

"Once this earth belonged to the Apache," Cochise said. His voice rose slightly. "Once the sun shined for the Apache. Once the rain fell for the Apache. Once the fruits and the wild animals lived for the Apache. The day has passed."

The men on the ground shifted in anger and bitterness.

"Now is the time to make a change," Cochise said. "Now is the time to learn the ways of the white man. Now is the time to find the way to peace. Otherwise the Apache will disappear from the earth as though he never was here."

There was more shifting and low cries of rage and some of the men raised their arms and shook them.

Cochise looked at the face of each man. "I have decided to make peace with the white man, to learn his ways, to live at his side."

Now some of the hunkered-down men cried out in disagreement. They cried out, "No, no, no . . ."

Cochise waited until they finished. "All who disagree with me are free to leave. All who remain will be bound by my word. Those who walk away, walk away now."

After a moment a man stood up. "I walk away."

Cochise's face was impassive.

A second man stood up. "I walk away."

A third followed and then a fourth. A fifth man rose.

The fifth man looked around. His face flooded with rage. "I walk away!" he shouted. "Who follows me?"

Presently another man rose and joined him.

"Who else?" the Indian demanded violently. "Who else joins me?"

None of the remaining men moved. Cochise looked at the small group who were leaving him.

"Take your belongings and take your people and leave," Cochise said. "You were my brothers but from now on you are my enemies. Do not set foot again on Chiricahua land. You will be slain."

The enraged man who had called out for followers strode up to Cochise. "I leave and I will leave behind my name. From now on I will be called by the name Mexican enemies call me. From now on I am Geronimo!"

He turned and stalked off. The other defectors followed. One of them paused and then returned to Cochise.

Cochise watched his fighting men leave him. His face was like stone.

Wesley called out, "Cut!" Then he said, "That was fine, print that." He stood up and looked around. "Well," he said. "I guess that winds it up."

The actors drifted off the set. The cameras and sound equipment were dismantled and taken away. Soon the clearing was empty. The picture making was ended.

Joe was unable to come back that quickly. He remained where he was, hunkered-down, and watched as the Chiricahua rancheria was taken apart, stripped. He felt sad but he did not know exactly why.

He thought about how much he needed of his past. He thought how he had had to listen to words written by white men, spoken by white men.

Where were the histories written by Apaches?

He got up and he felt tired and sad and he walked back to the reservation.

116

A few days later he went back to where the set had been. It was gone now, all of it. The wickiups were gone and the people were gone and it was as though none of it had happened.

The earth, the trees, the sky above, all had returned to today. The voices were gone. The people were gone. What had been the past, as truly as though a godlike hand had reached back and pulled it out, was gone. The world was a world of ghosts and the ghosts had departed.

He stood there and looked around and the sadness returned stronger than ever. Where were the histories written by Apaches?

Nineteen

Agent Lawton had returned and Hunter had brought him up-to-date on everything that had happened while he was gone. Lawton questioned the Deputy closely about the motion picture. At first he was a little concerned that the fighting scenes in the picture might have a bad effect on the Apaches but he dismissed that thought. In the end he was pleased that the Apaches were working and making a little extra money.

It was not long after the picture making was ended that Lawton learned in some way or another about the attempt Joe had made to get to his house on the night of the girl's coming-out party. He found out too about his Deputy's part in that incident and he summoned him to his office to question him about it.

Hunter shrugged. "It wasn't very much, Mr. Lawton," he said. He was surprised to find that the Agent had learned about the affair, but then, he told himself, he should have been surprised that Lawton had not heard about it earlier.

Lawton leaned back in his big chair and played with his riding crop. "What exactly was it, Bill?" His voice was polite.

Hunter knew about that polite voice. "You know, there was a lot of beer drinking. I guess Joe got a little souped up."

"And he started for my house. I thought I heard someone outside that night. What was his purpose, do you suppose?"

"He had this crazy idea," Hunter said. "He wanted to shake hands with you." That much was true, anyway.

Lawton sat forward, astonished. "Shake hands with me? What on earth for?"

Hunter shrugged. "Well, Mr. Lawton, you know, you once

118

asked him why he hadn't called on you when he got back and that must have stuck in his head. He had too much beer, I guess, and he had the notion he wanted to say hello and shake hands."

Lawton looked at Hunter hard. "That's preposterous. You know what time it was."

Hunter hunched his shoulders. "Like I say, Mr. Lawton, Joe was a little high. And Indians don't pay too much attention to time, you know that. They were dancing out there all night that night."

Lawton considered that. "Do you believe that's all he wanted to do, shake hands with me?"

"That's what he told me."

"Do you believe that?"

"I've got to go by what he said, Mr. Lawton. He didn't seem mad. He let me turn him around and point him back to the party."

"How did you get involved, Bill?"

Hunter felt he had to bend the truth a little. He didn't want to get Jennie Gates involved in this. If the Agent questioned her, and knowing Lawton, Hunter felt he might well do that, she might reveal deeper fears about what Joe might have done that night.

"I was out watching the dancers," Hunter said. "Winnie and I always try to catch those things. I happened to see Joe leave."

"And?"

"I saw him start toward your house and I went after him."

"Why?"

"It was pretty late. I figured you and Mrs. Lawton would be asleep."

"And?"

"I caught up with him and told him it was late and that you'd be happy to shake hands with him anytime."

"That was all?"

"Just about, sir."

"He never came around to shake my hand the next day. He never has."

Hunter said nothing.

"You don't think it was anything more than that?"

"No, sir."

Lawton got up and started pacing slowly in the office. "Why didn't you report this to me at the time?"

"An Indian with a little too much booze? It didn't seem all that important."

Lawton paused and faced him. "If you hadn't flagged him down it might have been quite important. Did you bother to consider that?"

On his way through the administration building Hunter paused at Jennie Gates' desk.

"Jennie, next time you see Joe, tell him Mr. Lawton knows about what happened that night—the night of the puberty ceremony. Tell Joe to take it easy. Tell him not to get himself in any trouble."

Twenty

It was hard to get back to the work on the range. It was hard for Joe and it was hard for Henry Sloane and it was hard for all the young men who had taken part in the film. In the days in which they had played the roles of their own ancestors the range had almost been forgotten. The old ways had come back easily and had filled them and this work on the range, this herding of cattle, this white man's work, had gone far away. For several days some of the men continued to call each other by the Indian names they had had in the film.

Joe worked hard and tried to put the picture out of his mind. He tried not to worry too much about what Jennie had told him, the warning the Deputy Agent had asked her to pass along. He didn't intend to get into any trouble but he also didn't think that mattered much. He knew the Agent wasn't just going to let it drop and that whether or not Joe made his own trouble the Agent would find some way to act against him.

He worked hard and he slept on the range most of the time and he behaved himself the best he could. He was grateful to Bill Hunter for tipping him off. He knew that the Agent must have questioned his Deputy and he knew too that the Deputy must have kept some things back or else the Agent would have done something right away.

But he knew no matter what he did it would not just pass. He knew he stood no chance against the Agent and against the power the Agent had. He knew that after the Agent thought about it for a while he would believe Joe had gone to his house that night for violence.

Meanwhile it was good to ride all day. After a while the memories of the days on the set faded away. This was reality again. The crunch of the saddle and the sweaty smell of the horse, the bleating of the calves, the bellowing of the steers and the smell of burned flesh when the Apache brand was put on. There was the horseplay among the young men and laughter and the talk of how they had all been Apache killers and how all that had become a joke. There was sitting around the fire at night with hot coffee and talk and the smell of the wood fire.

On the range the reservation seemed very far away. A man could even get to think he wasn't really on a reservation. After a few days even thoughts and fears about Agent Lawton seemed to get into perspective. After all, what could the Agent do? This was, after all, a free country, wasn't it?

At the end of the first week back on the range Joe went home for the first time. He hadn't seen his father all that week. His father had been working hard getting ready for the annual cattle sale and had had someone else take the tally for him.

When Joe got inside the house he had the feeling that his mother greeted him a little tightly. She looked worried. He took a shower and scrubbed himself clean and then he put on fresh clothes and went into the big kitchen. His father was working on books for the sale and just raised his head and nodded. The room seemed very quiet.

After a while the three of them ate dinner. Oliver Murdock filled his pipe. Joe looked closely at him.

"Is there anything wrong?" Joe asked.

"How was it out on the range?"

"The same. It's always good to be there."

"Yes. That's the best part of our lives."

Joe waited. "Is there anything wrong?" he asked again. All the good feeling of the range was in him but he began to feel it leak away. He began to have another kind of feeling.

122

Oliver Murdock puffed on his pipe. "There is always something wrong."

Joe looked over at his mother. She was ironing. She had cleared the table and had washed the dishes and now she was bent over the ironing board. She straightened and took the cooled iron to the stove and picked up a hot iron and returned to her work. She did not look at her husband or her son.

"What is wrong?" Joe asked. Slowly he began to know what it must be and his belly was sick. "Is it something serious?"

"It is always serious," Oliver Murdock said.

"Do you want to talk about it?" Joe asked.

Oliver drew on his pipe. Joe saw his mother glance up and then go back to her ironing.

"Does it have to do with the Agent?" Joe asked, feeling the sickness get worse.

"I don't know," Oliver said.

"You do know!" Florence Murdock said.

Joe looked at his mother in astonishment. He had never heard her speak to his father in that tone.

"I don't know," Oliver said. He eased his bad leg.

"Do you want to talk about it?" Joe asked again.

Oliver Murdock did not reply.

Florence Murdock turned to them again. "Mr. Linton has taken away our credit," she said.

Joe nodded. The sickness seeped slowly through all of him. He felt he should feel something more than sickness. He should feel surprise. He was not surprised.

The room was silent for a little while. Nobody wanted to say anything. Joe knew what this new move meant. It wasn't only money, having to have cash. He still had some army pay and there was the movie money. He had cash.

But it went deeper. When Linton cancelled credit it also

123

meant he wouldn't take cash. It meant he banned the Indian from the store.

But it went even deeper. To cut off an Indian's credit was to insult him. The Indian lost face. The family lost face. It was a public shaming.

"Why did he do that?" Joe asked. He knew, of course. He thought he knew.

"He did not say," Oliver Murdock said.

"He never says," Florence Murdock said, in that new voice Joe did not recognize.

"Maybe you can ask some of your friends to buy for you," Joe said. The words stuck in his craw.

"No," his father said. "Mr. Linton knows what people usually buy. He would find out. Then he would cancel their credit too."

Joe wondered if his parents knew about what happened the night of the puberty party. He was deeply ashamed of that by now. He told them about it.

His father nodded and did not say what he might have said. Instead he said quietly, "Maybe it was for that reason."

"It's the only reason," Joe said. "It's my fault."

"If that is the reason it is your fault," Oliver said. He was not angry. He was used to things.

Joe stood up and he felt the anger rising in him. He was angry at himself for his foolishness that night and he was angry with the Agent for taking this manner of revenge and he was angry at his father for accepting it meekly.

"There was no reason to punish my family," Joe said.

"There is nothing to be done," Oliver said.

Joe looked at his father bitterly. His father had bowed his head. His father belonged to the times when Indians bowed their heads.

"He's got to sell to you," Joe said. "He runs a public store. If you have the money he's got to sell to you."

124

Oliver took his pipe out of his mouth. "I would not go in there now. There would be no dignity in it."

Joe's shoulders sagged. He lowered his head. He was ashamed of himself again. His father thought in a way he did not think but his father still knew what was fitting and what was not.

Then it overwhelmed him. "That bastard!" he said. He clenched his hands hard. The hate and the pain filled him. "That bastard!" He looked at his father, at the bowed head, at the lame leg. "You'll just put up with it!" he shouted. "You'll just do nothing!"

"What can be done?" Oliver Murdock asked.

"Oh, *hell!*" Joe said. He held his hands so tight they hurt. He rushed out of the house.

Twenty-one

"Did he say where he was going?" Hunter asked.

Oliver Murdock shook his head. The Deputy Agent moved fast.

Oliver Murdock watched him hustle across the parade ground. Then Oliver limped over to the Council building. Nahilzay was there alone. Oliver sat down and talked to Nahilzay. He talked in Apache. He talked about many things. It was good to speak the old language. Oliver felt surer of himself in the old language.

Nahilzay held tightly to his war club and listened and did not reply. Oliver wondered whether Nahilzay was hearing what he was saying. Nahilzay just stared at the wall, seeing his vision.

When Hunter got across the parade ground he went into the administration building. It was just after quitting time. Some of the Bureau people were drifting out of the building. Hunter ran up the stairs and down the corridor to Lawton's office. He held his ear against the door. It was quiet inside the office. He knocked. There was no answer.

Hunter started away and then he was struck by the thought that maybe the Agent was unable to answer. He felt a chill. He went back. He hesitated for a moment and then he opened the door and went into the office. There was no one there.

Hunter hurried out of the building. He saw Jennie Gates still at her desk. He asked her if she had seen Joe.

She got that quick, frightened look. "No, Mr. Hunter, is there anything wrong?"

He shook his head and left the building. He started for the Agent's house. It was getting on to twilight now and when he reached the big house it seemed very quiet and he had the thought again, the fear, that it might be the last kind of quiet he wanted to find.

He stood still and tried to think. Mrs. Lawton would be there and if there had been any kind of trouble she would have let the world know about it. Just to make certain he reached out to ring the bell. He dropped his hand. What kind of excuse would he give if the Agent came to the door. *If* the Agent came to the door. He was thinking that way seriously now.

He went back to his office and telephoned Lawton. While he was dialing he thought how easy it was for him to believe Joe Murdock would do something violent.

Lawton answered the phone. Hunter realized the sweat was running down his back.

"Excuse me for disturbing you at home, Mr. Lawton," he said. "I was wondering whether you were finished with that bulletin that arrived from Washington."

"Why, yes, Bill, as a matter of fact I am."

"I wonder if I could have a look at it."

"Certainly, Bill. It's still on my desk. Go to my office and pick it up." The Agent sounded pleased.

"Thank you, sir." Hunter hung up. He ran to Lawton's office and got the directive. He went to his own office and put it on his desk and went out of the building again.

Where could Joe have gone? Now that it was over for the moment, now that he had spoken to the Agent, he acknowledged to himself he would not have been surprised at anything. It wasn't just Joe, he told himself. Any man whose family had been dealt a body blow like that might go wild. It wasn't just Joe, he told himself again.

Where could Joe have gone?

He went back to the Council building. He saw Judge Mel

Moore talking to Oliver Murdock. Moore told Hunter that Joe had borrowed the Council pickup and had gone off the reservation.

"Did he say where he was going?" Hunter asked. His mind was racing. Off the reservation could mean Arrowhead. Arrowhead could mean a saloon, booze.

"No," Judge Moore said. Then he said, "Oliver has told me what the sutler has done. It is unworthy of Mr. Lawton."

Hunter was thinking about a drunken Joe Murdock and the utterance of the Agent's name passed him for a moment. Then he said, "Mr. Lawton? It was Linton who closed the book."

Judge Moore walked away. He was a polite man and Hunter had considered him a friend but the Apache walked off.

Hunter looked at Oliver Murdock. He saw the tired misery on his face.

Twenty-two

Joe opened both windows of the pickup and let the night air come in. He sucked the air into his lungs. The anger was still in him. The anger and the frustration and the helplessness of his father had rubbed off on him and it made him feel shame.

It was another white night. The highway looked as though it was painted on the desert. How had it all come about? How had it come about they were prisoners on their own land? How had it come about they had to obey the orders of people who came there after them? People who had never conquered them.

The road was almost empty. He began to get the feeling he always got when he was away from the reservation alone. He felt free and he felt uneasy. Prison keeps things out as well as in.

Had Cochise been right? Was it wise to accommodate the white man? Was it right to learn the white man's style? It had preserved them as a people, true. They were alive and there was no killing, but was that everything? To be alive? There were many ways to die.

Supposing Cochise had decided otherwise and had fought until all the Chiricahua Apaches were dead. Then they would have gone with all the other peoples of the world who lived for a time and then vanished. Would that have not been better?

Death was never better. But there were so many ways to die. One could live and be dead.

Was it true that death was never better? Was death worse than that look on his father's face, knowing what must be going on inside his father's heart? Was death worse than hearing for the first time his mother speak in the voice that denied everything family meant?

Weren't all these things a kind of death?

Where was he going? He did not know. In the army he always knew where he was going. Where he was going when he was in the army did not always make sense to him and sometimes it was plainly stupid and often men were killed and wounded. But there was a purpose, he believed, however foolish it might seem. He always knew where he was going in Viet Nam.

He did not know now. He did not know especially at this moment at the wheel of the truck he had borrowed from the Council. Judge Moore, whose permission he had asked, had not questioned him.

He heard the hiss of the tires on the road and he took a deep breath of the fresh night air. He would like to just drive. He would like to drive for a long time and put as much country as he could between himself and the reservation. But he could not abandon his parents now.

He had brought dishonor upon his family because of his stupidity and he could not walk away from that.

What do white men do when they do not know where to go? White men always went to a saloon and got drunk and told the bartender all their troubles and the bartender always listened sympathetically. Bartenders were always wise and sympathetic. But only to white men. He could not imagine a bartender being sympathetic to an Apache Indian while he was getting drunk.

The night air seemed to smell of the cactus. It seemed like bitter perfume. It must have been a great time once. It must have been a great time and a great place. To be free on your own land and to live under your own law.

In a little while he saw the lights of Arrowhead. He drove

130

into the town, passing the used-car lot where he had once thought he could buy a truck. He passed the general store where the owner had once told him he would consider extending credit to Apaches. It had been pleasant then to think he could arrange these things. It had been foolish but it had been pleasant.

He parked the pickup and sat behind the wheel for a little while. He wondered about getting out of the truck like a free man and an ex-sergeant. He wondered about walking into a saloon and leaning on the bar, ordering a drink. The bartender would serve him, that was the law now, but it would not be like a white man leaning on the bar ordering a drink.

He thought about the Agent. Why had he not gone for the Agent this time?

Was it because he was a coward? Was it because he was afraid of going to jail, a real jail?

Was he a coward? He was not a coward during the fighting. Was this different? He did not know.

Maybe he was a coward. Or maybe it was just that he thought it would have done no good anyway. He could have done something to the Agent but what help would that have been?

Did this mean he was learning something? He did not know that either. He wished he had someone to talk to. There was no one.

He got down from the truck. He knew he had no anger against the Agent. He knew that what he felt went beyond anger into something else. What something else he did not know.

He walked down the street. People looked at him, or maybe he just thought that. It was dark and he was dressed like any other man. But he was not like any other man in Arrowhead. He did not belong in Arrowhead. He was alone in Arrowhead.

How much simpler it all would have been if he had been killed in Nam. He belonged to something there and he would have died where he belonged.

He saw a saloon. He started for it and then stopped. He felt a little frightened and he did not know why. He felt alone and frightened on this dusty street in this dusty Arizona town. He went to the door of the saloon and then he walked away from it. He could not that easily bring himself to go in and order a drink.

He walked beyond the saloon and then he paused. People looked at him. They looked at him casually, but they looked at him.

He started back for the saloon. Why shouldn't he go in and have a drink, like anybody else? He heard a car and he turned. It was a police car. The driver was looking at him. He walked past the saloon. He heard laughter inside through the open door.

He kept walking down the street. The police car followed alongside him. He had to hold himself in to keep from walking faster, running. The people on the street looked at him and at the police car.

He felt himself start to shake. He had done nothing. He had every right to walk on the street. He had more right maybe than many of the others.

The police car turned down a side street. He stopped walking. He was shaking. He saw people look at the shaking man.

He pulled himself together. The hell with them. The hell with all of them. He would like to shout to them that this was his country, that his people had been there long before their people had. He would like to tell them that he had worn their uniform for three years. But the hell with them.

He walked back to the saloon. He heard the laughter inside again. He couldn't make it. He knew when he walked in all the laughter would stop.

Twenty-three

It shouldn't be too hard to find out, Hunter thought. There weren't that many bars in Arrowhead. Three, maybe four. And then there was the local clink.

He pulled his car up to the curb and got out. He kept his eye open for the Council pickup. He didn't see the truck anywhere. He went into the saloons and spoke to the bartenders. Joe hadn't been to any of the places. The bartenders were sure of that. They'd have remembered if an Indian had come in. There weren't that many Indians who went into saloons.

Hunter went to the sheriff's office. Nothing. There had been no trouble. The man on duty wanted to know who Hunter was looking for. Hunter said it didn't matter. He said if there was no Apache in jail it didn't matter. The man on duty asked again just who he was looking for and just what he thought might have happened but Hunter wouldn't give him any more.

Hunter went back to his car. Now what? If Joe was going to get loaded he'd have come to Arrowhead. The next town was miles beyond.

He got into the car and drove around the town slowly looking for the pickup. There was no sign of it. He drove into a gas station and had the tank filled.

Where could Joe be? He could have bought a bottle and gone off somewhere to finish it. There were a number of places where he could have bought a bottle. He thought about going to each place and asking. He couldn't do that. He couldn't walk into a store and ask whether an Indian had bought a bottle of booze.

133

He paid for the gas and started back for the reservation. He tried to put himself into Joe Murdock's place. What would he do if he were Joe Murdock? He drove slowly and tried to think. He tried to remember Joe's touchstones. He felt something wandering around inside his head, a message, something. He tried to read it. He couldn't.

He drove and he tried to think and he couldn't and he wanted to hit something, pound on something in his bafflement, and he thought how easy it was to lash out, to strike, when you were balked. Then he passed a crossroad and it came to him and he let out a shout.

He stopped the car, backed up, turned into the crossroad. He drove for about fifteen minutes and then he slowed as he rounded a big curve where the highway cut through a hill.

He saw him in the distance. He jammed on the brakes, and switched off his headlights.

The Cochise profile lay in a soft, white, furry glow from the moon. The face seemed alive, even more alive than it had that night when he had taken Joe there. The face seemed alive and listening.

Joe was standing in the road, staring at the face etched against the sky. He stood fixed as a statue.

Hunter was thankful Joe hadn't heard him drive up. He left the car lights off and backed away slowly. He turned the wheels. He tried to make as little sound as possible. Perhaps it wouldn't have mattered. Joe was somewhere else. He drove away.

Joe gazed at the profile. Slowly he raised his arms.
"Teach me," he said. "Give me to know."

Twenty-four

It was another dry, broiling day. Heat waves rose in shimmers from the shining hoods of the used cars. Al Adams rolled his cigar from one side of his mouth to the other.

"Sorry, Sarge," he said. "Them trucks is gone. And they were lulus. Real clean, you know what I mean?"

Joe said, "I don't want a truck, Mr. Adams. I can't afford a truck."

Adams waved his hand expansively. "Look around, Sarge. Looking don't cost nothing. Looking is free."

He cast his eyes about the lot for other buyers. He had lost interest in Joe.

"I want something cheaper," Joe said. "Have you got a jeep?"

Joe felt the wave of nervousness again. He had wakened that morning knowing what he must do and he had hitched a ride from the reservation and now he was trying to do it but he was scared again. He had prayed for guidance and sometime during the night it had been given to him. He had had a vision, the way Nahilzay had visions. He did not remember the moment of the vision but when he opened his eyes he knew he had been informed. But now he was scared. What he was doing was a big thing.

Adams was interested again. "A jeep, Sarge? As a matter of fact, I have."

He took Joe by the arm and led him through the forest of cars. "There," he said. "There you are. And it's clean, you know what I mean? Real clean, Sarge. I wouldn't try to fool a pro like you."

135

Joe looked over the jeep carefully. He had spent three months once working in a motor pool in a Southern army camp and he knew a little something. When Al Adams saw the way he was checking things out he cut off his spiel and just watched him.

A little while later Joe straightened. "How much?"

"You can see for yourself, Sarge, it's a clean lulu."

"How much?"

"Twelve."

"Twelve?"

"One thousand two."

"I'll think about it," Joe said. He started to walk out of the lot.

"It's clean, Sarge," Al Adams said. "Don't think too long. Remember those trucks. Clean lulus don't last."

"I'll think on it," Joe said, still walking. He was very scared. Twelve hundred dollars . . .

Al Adams caught up with him. "Wait a minute, Sarge. Don't you know the rules?"

Joe looked to the right and left. He felt hemmed in again and he wanted to make sure he had a way out.

Al Adams chewed on his cigar. "I tell you a price it's just for openers. I said twelve. Now you got to make me a counter offer. Don't you know how to bounce the ball?"

"No," Joe said.

Adams took off his big Stetson and wiped his forehead. "You interested in this jeep, Sarge?"

"Maybe."

"It's clean, ain't it?"

"Looks like."

Adams put his hand on Joe's shoulder. "Come into my office, Sarge. It ain't so hot in there."

An hour later Joe owned the jeep. He and Adams had settled on a thousand and fifty dollars. Joe paid cash.

136

"You have any problems you come back here, Sarge."

Joe nodded.

"Don't want no Indian uprising," Al Adams said. "Specially not with no Apache who was in Viet Nam."

He laughed and Joe drove away. He drove down the main street of Arrowhead to the general store. The owner frowned for a moment, trying to remember where he had seen Joe before. Then he asked Joe what had happened to that idea they had had.

"Nothing," Joe said. He told the man what he wanted. Some stewing meat. Canned food. Some flour. Coffee. Sugar. Tobacco for his father. He looked around for something special for his mother. He didn't know what his mother would like. He finally chose a jar of blackberry jam. He bought white bread to put the jam on.

The man put everything into a paper sack and Joe paid him.

"I liked that idea we spoke about," the man said. "What happened?"

"Nothing."

"I'd like to talk more. I'd like to do business with you people. It might have been a good idea you had."

"It might have been," Joe said.

He started back for the reservation. He felt good driving the jeep that belonged to him and he still felt scared. He had never bought a car before. He had never bought anything as expensive as that before. He had never spent that kind of money. It was more than that. It was more than buying a car and spending the movie money.

On the way back the good feeling began to drain off as he realized the size of the thing he had done. He had bought a car the way he might have bought a pack of cigarettes. Not quite, but almost. It was more. He had defied the Agent. He had pitted himself against the establishment, against the

137

rules. He knew about rules. The last three years of his life had been lived according to the rules. He knew what happened to people who broke the rules.

He knew that when he had learned the Agent had found out what happened the night of the puberty ceremony he should have gone to him. Hat in hand he should have apologized. Then the Agent would have smiled and he would have forgiven him the way he would forgive any thoughtless child. Then it would have ended at that and the Agent would not have punished his parents, through Linton. That was the way it should have happened. That was the drill.

Instead he hadn't done that at all and his parents had been disgraced and now he was making it worse.

All the courage that had sustained him through buying the jeep was run out as he drove onto the reservation. He felt frightened and guilty. He felt almost as though he had stolen the jeep and the bag of food.

He saw people turn and look at him as he drove past the parade ground. There were not many cars on the reservation, almost no cars owned by Indians. Joe knew that before he reached his house everybody in the Bureau would know he had driven in in a jeep and that before long the Agent would know it too.

Florence Murdock was sitting on the front porch shucking peas as Joe drove up. She raised her head and then she was puzzled and then she just looked worried. She looked around to see whether any of the neighbors were watching.

The sound of the jeep brought Oliver out of the house. His face tightened.

His parents' reaction drove away Joe's own fear. He hated to see how frightened they were and it made him mad. His father came down from the porch. Oliver looked over the jeep and then he looked at the bag of supplies. Oliver's face was still and he knew his father was retreating the way he retreated. Oliver touched the side of the jeep.

138

"Did you borrow this from a friend?" Oliver Murdock asked. He looked around too, to see if anybody else was looking at all this.

"I bought it," Joe said.

"You decided that by yourself." Oliver Murdock's voice was dead.

"I didn't ask the Agent's permission, if that's what you mean," Joe said. He was sorry he said that. He saw his father recoil slightly as though he had been flicked with a whip. "It was my money, Pop. I earned it."

Now some of the other people who lived around there were drifting over. Oliver said nothing.

"I worked for that money," Joe said. "Everybody keeps telling me it's a free country."

Oliver saw the other people gathering round. He backed away. He wanted to disassociate himself from the jeep. Joe looked at his mother. She was still on the porch. She had stopped shelling peas. She was looking at the people gathering around. There were only about half a dozen or so but they seemed like a crowd.

Joe reached into the bag. "Pop, I bought you some tobacco." He held out the tin.

Oliver Murdock put his hands behind his back.

Joe looked at him and then at the people. "It's the kind you smoke. Please, Pop."

Oliver kept his hands clasped behind his back.

Joe reached into the bag and took out the jar of blackberry jam. "Look, Mom, I bought this for you."

Mrs. Murdock raised her head and shivered.

Joe held the tobacco tin in one hand and the jam jar in the other. He looked at his parents and then at the other people and then back at his parents. "Pop, Mom, what were we supposed to do? Starve? If Linton won't sell us food we have to get it somewhere else, don't we?"

139

Nobody said anything.

"I didn't steal this!" Joe shouted. "I bought it! I worked for the money and I bought it!"

After a little while Oliver Murdock said in a low voice, "It was not the right thing."

Joe's arms dropped. "What was the right thing, Pop? To go and kiss Lawton's boot?" He closed his eyes. "I'm sorry, Pop." He held out the tobacco tin. "Please take it, Pop. Please, I bought it for you."

Oliver Murdock looked at his friends and neighbors.

"Please, Pop," Joe said.

Oliver Murdock looked around again and then he accepted the tin. Nobody said anything.

Joe put the blackberry jam back into the sack. He jumped down from the jeep. He looked at it. It looked strong. He needed to know that. He touched it. The metal was hot from the sun. It was hot and hard and unyielding and unafraid to be touched.

"It's nice, isn't it, Pop?" he asked.

"It does not belong here," Oliver said. He went up the steps into the house. He held the tobacco tin close to him, as though to try to hide it.

Joe lifted the paper sack of supplies out of the jeep. Sam Hopkins came up and walked around the jeep, inspecting it. It made Joe feel better for some reason, maybe it was because Sam Hopkins had also been in the army.

"GI?" Sam asked.

"I don't think so," Joe said.

"Looks good."

"That's what the man said."

Sam Hopkins looked into the paper sack. "Goods?"

"Yes."

"From Arrowhead?"

"Yes."

There was a murmuring among the other people.

"Heard about Linton, what he did," Sam Hopkins said. He kicked one of the jeep tires. "This looks good."

Joe walked up the three steps to the porch. They were three long steps. He used to jump them. He saw the look on his mother's face as he carried the bag inside.

The neighbors didn't go away. They stood in the sun and looked at the jeep.

Oliver Murdock pushed his plate away. "I've had enough."

"You ate hardly anything," Florence Murdock said.

"I've had enough."

"It's good beef," Joe said. "The man said it was good beef. It tastes good to me."

"I've had enough," Oliver said.

The evening meal, made mostly of food Joe had brought back from Arrowhead, had been eaten in silence. There never was too much talk. It went back a long time to when Apaches had to eat quickly and silently, to the time when they never knew when a meal would be interrupted. That was the way it was, except for feasts. This was not a feast.

Oliver and Florence Murdock had barely tasted the food. Joe was sore at seeing them so frightened. It spoiled his appetite too. He knew he was also a little frightened and that didn't help.

What the hell was it? He wanted to yell out. What had he done? What had he really done?

He saw his father take out his pipe. He saw his father look around for his tobacco. Joe got up and brought him the tin he had bought in Arrowhead.

"Here, Pop," he said.

Oliver looked at the tin. He looked at it for a long time. Then he took it from Joe and broke the seal and opened the top and scooped out some tobacco with his forefinger. Joe

141

felt suddenly so good he wanted to yell. Or maybe what he wanted to do was to cry, for this, for everything else that was going on.

He watched his father fill the pipe and tamp down the tobacco with his thumb and then strike a wooden match. It would not have surprised Joe if the tobacco didn't light. It would not have surprised him if by some secret power the Agent could prevent the tobacco from taking. It would not have surprised him if the tobacco had exploded in his father's face.

When Oliver Murdock was exhaling a thick cloud of smoke Joe was so relieved he couldn't believe it.

After a little while there was a knock on the door and Sam Hopkins came in.

"I looked at the jeep again," Sam said.

Oliver, resting his bad leg, looked up nervously. He blew out smoke as though to hide himself from this talk.

"I used to drive one," Sam Hopkins said.

"You can drive this one."

"Maybe I forgot."

"You never forget," Joe said.

Presently Sam Hopkins said, "The next time you go to Arrowhead . . ."

"Yes," Joe said.

"Maybe you could take me along," Sam Hopkins said. "I haven't been there in a long time."

"Sure," Joe said.

Oliver Murdock puffed on his pipe. Florence was mending a pair of levis.

"I haven't been there in a long time," Sam said again. "Not since I last got some cattle money."

"Probably nothing's changed," Joe said.

"They have good things there, I remember," Sam said. "Things don't cost as much. Maybe I could buy some goods there too."

"They want cash," Oliver said.

"I did some work on that movie," Sam Hopkins said. "I have a little cash."

When Joe and Sam Hopkins drove off the reservation three or four days later Sam's lips were tight. Joe knew that look. He had seen that look on the faces of men going into battle.

The look stayed on Sam Hopkins' face clear across the parade ground and through the reservation gate and onto the state highway. It didn't go away until they were halfway to Arrowhead. Then Sam started to whistle and it went away.

Twenty-five

Lawton chuckled. "He probably won't be able to keep up the payments. They'll undoubtedly have to come here to repossess that jeep."

"I understand he paid for it in full," Bill Hunter said. "From the movie money he made."

"Ah, yes, that movie money," Lawton said. "Well, when he runs out of that windfall he'll find himself in trouble. Gas. Tires. Repairs. Upkeep. Insurance. These Indians are so irresponsible. They never think about things like that."

Hunter found himself asking, "Why are you so against him, Mr. Lawton? It can't be for that one night he got himself looped. You couldn't hold that against him forever."

Hunter had never dared question his superior that way before and he wondered what had made him do it now. He knew the Agent didn't like to be asked direct questions by his subordinates.

But Lawton didn't seem to mind this time. He fiddled with his riding crop and then he used a word Hunter hadn't heard for a long time and which the Deputy couldn't quite believe.

"He's uppity," Lawton said.

Hunter lit a cigarette to cover his surprise. That word just wasn't used anymore, not even against blacks, except as a bad joke.

Lawton looked up from his desk. His face was quite serious. "Someday, Bill, if all goes well with you, you may find yourself in the position of being Agent, with all the responsibility of the office, with so many people depending on your judgment and good sense. You'll discover, if you're fit for your post, that you don't think of individuals but of the people as a whole, of the tribe. Not what is good for one person but what is best for everyone."

He got up from the desk and walked to the window and looked out. The light outlined his profile. It was, Hunter thought, a fine, well-bred profile.

"You think of what's good for the tribe," the Agent said. "The tribe. The tribe as a whole. What's good for them and what's bad for them. Nothing else. And one single trouble-maker can create an extraordinary amount of harm. One rotten apple. Not to us. Not to the Bureau. But to his own people." He turned to Hunter. "It is my duty, Bill, just as in a similar situation it would be your duty as Agent, to make certain that Joe Murdock does not do this damage to his people. Even if it causes him to suffer personally."

Hunter knew Lawton believed in what he said. Lawton had been an agent for a long time and he had his own kind of integrity and principle. Hunter knew of many agents of Lawton's era who believed very much the same way. Actually it was a big step when they considered Indians as children. It wasn't long ago they regarded them as scarcely more than animals.

Lawton went back to his desk. He picked up the crop and held it between his hands. "Of course, it's always possible Murdock may see the error of his ways. If he ever convinces me of that I shall use my influence with Mr. Linton to persuade him to restore credit to the family."

Twenty-six

"Do you know my name?" The man who ran the general store in Arrowhead looked at Joe and then at Sam Hopkins.

"No," Joe said. He thought it was an unnecessary question.

"You two have been coming here for two–three weeks now and you still don't know my name," the man said.

"No," Joe said. He wondered what this was all about. He felt uneasy.

"Don't you want to know the name of the man you're doing business with?" the man asked.

"We pay cash," Joe said.

"I know your name."

Joe backed off a little. It was bad when someone had personal information about you, especially when you had none about him. It gave the other man a power over you. He had your name in his pocket.

"Your name is Joe Murdock," the man said. "I checked on you."

Joe backed away a little more. He began to feel closed in again. "I pay cash," he said.

"You're a war hero," the man said. "I know all about you. Why don't you talk about those things. People would like to hear about it."

Joe didn't have any answer to that. He picked up a sack filled with supplies and started out of the store. Sam Hopkins picked up a couple of more bags. The owner of the store followed them out to the jeep.

"Don't you like to do business with me?" the man asked.

"Yes," Joe said.

"My name is Woody Rogers. You never asked."

Joe stowed the bag in the back and stepped back for Sam Hopkins to put in the other bags.

"Where are the rest of you?" Woody Rogers asked.

"The rest of who?" Joe asked. He got into the jeep, behind the wheel. He wanted to be able to get away. He didn't like this kind of questioning. He bought what he needed and Sam Hopkins bought what he needed and they paid for it and there was no need for questions.

"The other Indians on the reservation. Where are your friends? I give you fair prices," Rogers said.

Joe started the motor.

"That other time you spoke to me about other people," Rogers said. He was leaning inside the jeep and he didn't move even when the motor started. "You told me there might be others who'd trade with me."

"I thought about that once," Joe said.

"What happened? I told you I wanted to think about it. We never talked about it again."

"Things happened," Joe said.

"What's stopping it now?"

"Those people don't always have cash. They usually don't have cash. Most of them get money only after we sell beeves."

"I know all about that. I know all about Linton. I know all about how Linton gives credit. You people have a pretty good track record. I know about that."

Rogers stepped back. Joe nodded and drove off.

On the way back to the reservation, Sam Hopkins asked, "You know Malloy? Fat Malloy?"

"Yes."

"He was asking me just the other day."

"Asking you what?"

"Whether we could buy for him and his family. That Fat Malloy, he eats a lot. His wife is just as fat as he is."

After a while Sam Hopkins asked, "What's the matter with you?"

"Why?" Joe asked.

"You have a funny look on your face."

"I'm thinking."

"Don't do that while you're driving." Sam sat back in his seat. He looked out. Riding in the cutaway jeep was riding in the open. Everything outside was close. "You know something, Joe?"

"What?"

"I don't feel funny anymore."

"Funny?"

"The first time we went to Arrowhead together. I felt funny. You know, funny."

"Like the Agent was going to call out the police to stop us."

"By God, no, not that! Yes, by God, that! Something like that." He turned to Joe. "How did you know that?"

"I felt the same way in the beginning."

"By God." Sam Hopkins stared at the desert rolling by. "It's a shame. This food is good. It's fresh. It costs less. Maybe we ought to help Fat Malloy. It's a shame lots of people can't get the benefit. It's a shame the Council doesn't do something." He looked at Joe. "Hey, you thinking again?"

Joe nodded.

"It does this bad thing to your face," Sam said.

"The Council is made of old women."

"I agree. Maybe it is only because no one but you can hear me but I will not disagree. Or maybe it's because I feel good. I will not disagree."

"The Council will do nothing. The Council is afraid to make the Agent mad."

148

"Agreed. By God, agreed. Hey, stop thinking so hard. Your face is terrible."

When they were back on the reservation Joe went over to the Tribal Council building and got hold of a copy of the Tribal Charter. He got it from Judge Mel Moore who didn't ask why he wanted it. Joe studied the document. He decided that, like all such pieces of legislation, it was open to interpretation. It depended on who had the clout at any given time. He read the clauses over and over again. It was like probing for weak spots in the enemy line.

When he got back to his house he found Sam Hopkins waiting for him. With Sam was Fat Malloy. Fat Malloy was not much older than Sam but his fat made him look older. He told Joe Sam had said there was a chance he might trade in Arrowhead on credit.

"Don't start thinking too hard," Sam said to Joe. "You'll frighten Fat Malloy with that face."

"Sam said the man in Arrowhead was ready to give credit," Fat Malloy said again.

"Until after the cattle sale," Joe said. "You aren't working the herd."

"My sons are," Fat Malloy said. "I have three sons."

"That's true," Joe said. He went into the house and asked his father for permission to look into the tally book. The three Malloy boys had substantial money coming to them.

"I'll try it for you," Joe said. "But it's my word I'll be giving."

"I will not break your word," Fat Malloy said.

The next morning Fat Malloy was back with a list of things he needed. With him was Henry Sloane, the young brave Joe had tangled with. He had a list for his family. There was another man, Johnny Redleather. He had a list too.

"You'll see molasses on the list," Johnny Redleather said. "Old Linton never carries nothing but sorghum. My woman likes molasses, if you can get it."

149

Joe said, "I wasn't going to Arrowhead for a couple of days. I went there yesterday."

Fat Malloy and Henry Sloane and Johnny Redleather all looked disappointed. But none of them would say anything. None of them would urge.

"I don't want to make money on you," Joe said. "But gasoline costs."

"We will pay you for the gasoline," Johnny Redleather said immediately. "And for your time too. You should not be doing this for nothing. It would have no dignity. Please try to find real molasses."

Oliver Murdock listened and shook his head. He felt there was a conspiracy going on in his house and he did not like it.

Sam Hopkins insisted on going along with Joe. In the Arrowhead store Joe signed his name for Fat Malloy and Johnny Redleather and Henry Sloane. He saw when the bills were totted up that Woody Rogers took off a small percentage.

"The more customers you bring the more discount I'll give to all of you," Rogers said. "It's only right."

He gave Joe sales slips for the buyers so they'd have receipts to compare with the bills when they were presented after the cattle sales.

On the way home, Joe said, "I've been thinking."

"It does not look well on you."

"What do you do with your life?"

"I work. I work hard."

"You are respected."

"I believe so."

"You were a warrior."

"Not like you."

"I am young. You are a respected man."

"What are you saying?"

"Who represents you on the Tribal Council?"

150

"I don't know."

"You don't know."

"I said that. Who cares about the Council. The Council does nothing for me."

"Hiram Peterson."

"Hiram? I'll be damned."

"He has represented our district for twelve years."

"I'll be damned."

"Didn't you vote for him?"

"No."

"Why not?" Joe asked.

"What's the Council. The Council does nothing."

"What has Hiram Peterson done for you?"

"Nothing. I told you, by God, nothing."

"Why don't you run for his seat this time?"

"Nothing, by God, nothing. Hiram Peterson has done nothing for me or my family. Twelve years. By God." He twisted around in his seat. "What crazy thing did you say?"

"Why don't you run for the Council for our district?"

"Me?"

"Why not? You are respected."

"What do I know about that stuff?"

"All you got to do is beat a man who's been there twelve years and you didn't even know his name."

Twenty-seven

Within a couple of weeks another ten or twelve families asked Joe to trade for them. He checked their time in the tally book and then he took their orders. It was what he had planned in the beginning, when he wanted to buy a truck. Now it was coming to him without his doing anything about it.

He took the orders and he talked politics. He asked the people about their representatives on the Council. He asked them what their councilmen had done for them. Most of the people couldn't answer him.

"The Council has been the same for years," Joe said. "Maybe it's time for a little change."

The men listened to him. At first he had been hesitant to speak to them because they were older than he was and he had no status in the tribe, except maybe as somebody who got into trouble. But they listened to him and when he found that out, his confidence grew. He guessed they listened to him out of politeness, since they were polite by nature, and also because he was buying supplies for them and saving them money.

It went beyond this but he didn't know that. It went to something deeply Apache. The Apaches were in history a warrior people and at this moment in time Sgt. Joe Murdock was the only real warrior around.

An old Apache, a man who still wore his hair long and banded around the forehead, gave Joe a shopping list and asked him if he could read it. Joe looked at the list and nodded.

152

"My old woman wrote it down," the old man said. "She remembers to write better than I do."

"I can read it," Joe said.

"What is this you are talking about? About new councilmen?" The old man leaned against the jeep.

"I think new councilmen would be a good thing," Joe said.

"What difference would it make? New councilmen would be the same as old councilmen."

"Then nothing would be lost. But maybe they would be different."

"Do you think that?"

"It might be."

"Are you sure you can read what's on the list?"

"Yes."

"You may be right. New men might be different but I doubt that. Do you speak for any man?"

"No."

Oliver Murdock saw a lot of this and heard some of it. He didn't like any of it.

"Why are you talking to the people?" he asked Joe. "What do you know about politics and the Council?"

"Nothing."

"Then why do you try to stir up trouble?"

"We're supposed to pick men of our own choice, aren't we? That's what the Charter says, doesn't it?"

Oliver Murdock had to admit that was true.

"It's supposed to teach us how to be good democratic Americans, isn't it?"

Oliver nodded.

"Then all I'm doing is following the Charter," Joe said.

"It won't end well," his father said.

Although Joe was not secretive about his political talks with the people, the men he spoke to, from an ancient lack of faith in anything new, sensed they must think privately on what Joe had said and not repeat it to anyone else.

That was why the Agent never heard anything. The Deputy Agent heard nothing, although he was closer to some Apaches than the Agent was, and up to now Joe had talked to him freely.

The Agent did hear how Joe's business was growing and that confounded him. It contradicted everything he believed about Indians and the things they were capable of doing.

Lawton thought about it for a long time. It troubled him to have fundamental beliefs challenged this way. He finally found an explanation that suited him. He explained it to Bill Hunter.

"It was the army," the Agent said.

"How do you figure that, Mr. Lawton?"

"Whatever savvy he has, whatever know-how, he learned from Uncle Sam," the Agent said. "Indians can't think things out that way all by themselves."

The Agent smiled comfortably. He was pleased he had reasoned this out. He could still hold on to his beliefs.

Twenty-eight

In the old days there was a ceremony before the cattle sales. The people would gather and the shaman would make reverence to the four directions and give thanks to The Everywhere Spirit for the good things of the year. The people would celebrate with the shaman and give their own thanks for the money they would have to face the hard winter ahead.

The Apaches had got away from that now, more or less, although a small prayer of thanksgiving was still given by a holy man and some of the older people joined him. But whether Apaches were there to listen to the shaman or not there was a feeling of gratitude in the hearts of all of them. They had worked hard for months on the dusty, harsh range, they or their husbands or their sons or their brothers, and now they would reap the benefit of their labors.

When they saw the big Cadillacs and Lincolns pull up in front of the administration building, when they saw the men in their big hats and embroidered boots get out, smelling of good bourbon and fine cigars, they rejoiced.

There were certain formalities. Courtesies were exchanged between the buyers and the Agent and the members of the Tribal Council. They drank toasts to each other and cigars were passed around. After that the buyers were provided with horses and they rode out to the range to look at the cattle. The buyers did that as a formality. They knew by now that Apache beef was top quality.

On the range Joe watched the men mosey around the steers. It was the first time he had been on the range during the sales. He watched his father limping along with the buyers as they made their inspection. The buyers were respectful to Oliver Murdock. Joe was a little surprised to see that much respect, and then right away he felt ashamed of himself for feeling surprised his father was respected, and after that he was glad and proud his father was held in such esteem.

For the time the buyers were there Oliver Murdock seemed to change. He had power and he had authority. When the buyers joked with him about prices and told him he was holding them up, it was understood by everyone that it was just a joke. The buyers knew they had to pay top dollar. The buyers knew they couldn't fool around with Oliver Murdock. He knew his job and he knew values.

That made the joking a good thing. It meant the white men and his father were chaffing with each other as equals. His father took on an honor Joe had never seen before. It made Joe feel better than he had ever felt. It made him feel proud of his father and that was the finest feeling of all.

One of the buyers, a tall, skinny man with a face like leather, pushed back his Stetson one afternoon and looked at the milling steers.

"I still can't get over it," he said to Joe. "I been coming here ten–twelve years now and I still can't get over it."

"What is it you can't get over?" Joe asked politely, although he was pretty sure he knew.

"Apaches raising beef," the man said, shaking his head. "It just don't seem real. When my great-granddaddy started ranching here . . ." He stopped short.

"The Apaches stole cattle instead of raising it," Joe finished for him.

"Well, you know," the man said. He seemed a little embarrassed. "Well, things were a little different then, weren't they? You told my great-granddaddy that one day I'd be buying Apache beef and shipping it along with my own he'd have had my head examined."

156

Joe nodded.

"Still and all, he helped start all this," the man said. He took out a long, thin, bent cheroot and lit it. "He gave old Cochise some breeding stock then, along with the others." He laughed. "Not because he was charitable, understand. He just wanted Cochise off his neck, like all the other ranchers." He laughed again. "He figured it was better to give them away than to have them lifted." He looked at the cattle. "Some of them beeves there, some of them we're looking at right now, might have come down from my great-grand-daddy's herd."

Joe turned his eyes to the cattle and then to the man and he felt a little chill go through him on that warm, sunny day. It brought it all close together, the man and his family, and Joe and his ancestors, and the animals and Cochise, all in a line, all connected.

"Well, it turned out a good thing," the man said. He slapped Joe on the back and moved on.

After the sales were over the white wranglers arrived and drove the steers away. Joe watched them move along, shambling, bellowing, and after they were gone everything looked empty. The range seemed empty. It wasn't really. There was plenty of stock left to be readied for next year, but it looked empty. It looked the way the land looked after the moving-picture company went away. It was, he knew, because in each case a part of his life had ended too.

After the money was paid over to the Tribal Council, Oliver Murdock opened the year's book, and the work hours were added up on a machine the Council borrowed from the Bureau and each man was given his proper share.

As always, before they did anything else, the people settled with the sutler, Linton. This time there was a small addition. Joe Murdock's customers gave him money to settle with Woody Rogers in Arrowhead.

157

The money that was left over was husbanded carefully. Repairs were made on houses. Tools were fixed or maybe replaced. Women might invest in new Mother Hubbards if the old ones were worn out. Men bought boots and levis and checkered shirts. There was winter in the air and some of the people bought outer clothing.

Linton's store was very busy.

However little money was left after the necessities, parents always bought something for the little children. Cattle sale time was like Christmas at San Pedro. It was as though Santa Claus' sled was pulled around by steers.

Twenty-nine

Late on the evening of election day Sam Hopkins came round to the Murdock house. He seemed bewildered.

"I can't believe it," he said. "They elected me."

Joe took a deep breath. He would have to look at Sam Hopkins in a different way now. Sam Hopkins had gone back and forth to Arrowhead with him, he had been an assistant, so to speak, but now he was a member of the Tribal Council.

"Congratulations," Joe said.

"I still don't believe it," Sam Hopkins said.

Oliver Murdock didn't congratulate Sam Hopkins. He had the built-in fear that changes weren't good. The Tribal Council had been the same for a long time. Nobody had ever challenged the members. Along with other Apaches Oliver considered politics a white man's game and not altogether honest. Oliver suspected change. Change was uncertain. What you were used to, good or bad, was safer. Beyond that he had the Indian feeling that to kick a man out of office was an insult. He wondered how he would be able to face Hiram Peterson, the councilman Sam Hopkins had replaced. Hiram Peterson probably would now hear about the way Joe had been talking and that made it worse.

Besides Sam Hopkins, two other new councilmen were elected. They were elected by small margins, as Sam Hopkins had been, but they were elected. They ousted men who had been in office so long they hadn't bothered to go around and speak to the voters.

All the time that Joe had been talking about getting some

159

new blood into the Council another idea had been growing in his mind. He had never mentioned it to anyone, not even to Sam Hopkins. It was so important he wanted to think on it for a long time by himself. He knew that to talk about something often diluted it or tainted it. He could not even say when the idea had first come to him. It had come along, little by little, on those long trips back and forth from Arrowhead, he guessed.

At first the idea had been so stunning, so revolutionary, it scared him. He had thought he must be crazy. He put it out of his mind and tried to forget it but it kept coming back, and each time it came back it had more size. It bounced around in his head like a hot potato and then after a while it didn't seem so crazy and it didn't frighten him.

The new Tribal Council had its first meeting about a week after the elections. The three new members were a little uncomfortable taking their seats for the first time. None of them had had anything to do with tribal affairs before.

They were awkward, and not knowing what to do they turned instinctively to Nahilzay who, as always, was seated alone. The ancient warrior said nothing. He did not acknowledge their presence. But they got something from him. One of the newcomers touched the war staff. Sam Hopkins stroked the eagle feathers. Nahilzay remained impassive but he did not stop them.

Lester Matthews, as presiding officer, opened the meeting. Previously Lester Matthews had had a long talk with the Agent. The Agent was shocked by the change made in the Council. He considered it revolutionary. Lester Matthews had reassured him. He had told the Agent all would be as it was before.

Lester Matthews started off the meeting by being condescending to the three new men. He told them they must have

160

great, special talents to have been elected by the people to replace the three wise and experienced men who had preceded them.

Then in the midst of this kind of talk Lester Matthews had sudden second thoughts. He realized that the three new men were councilmen now and each would have a vote equal to anyone else's vote. He shifted gears and began to flatter the newcomers. He tried hard to sound sincere.

The new men replied in kind. They told Lester Matthews how proud they were to serve with him, a man of such wisdom. During this Nahilzay made a small shift in his seat although that might have had nothing to do with the fulsome compliments being exchanged.

The men were still singing each other's praises and probably would have filled the meeting doing nothing else when the door opened and Joe Murdock walked in. Lester Matthews, at that moment listening to Sam Hopkins describe him as one of the great Apache statesmen of all time, reluctantly pounded his gavel.

"What do you want here?" he asked Joe. "The Council is conducting serious business."

"I will speak," Joe said.

"On what authority?" Lester Matthews asked.

Joe cleared his throat and braced himself. "Paragraph two, section six of the bylaws of the Charter of the San Pedro Reservation," he said. " 'Any bona fide member of the tribe has the right to address the Council at any regularly scheduled meeting.' " Joe paused.

Lester Matthews, who boasted far and wide that he knew the Charter by heart, chapter and verse, could do nothing now but nod. "Speak out then," he said in his finest official voice. "The Council will listen."

Now that he was there, now that he was about to talk about what had been wheeling around and around in his head for so many weeks, Joe didn't feel sure of himself. The idea he had conceived, had nurtured, had worried over like a mother hen, didn't seem all that valid just then.

"Get on with it," Lester Matthews said. "The Council has important matters to consider."

"I will be quick," Joe said, stalling. "I have something to say. I ask the Council to think on it."

"Get on with it," Lester Matthews said again.

Now Joe took that deep breath. There was a considerable part of him that regretted his coming before the Council. "We all know about the general store and the way it is run by the sutler Linton."

Lester Matthews frowned and leaned forward a little. The other councilmen, including Sam Hopkins, looked puzzled.

"I will not take the Council's time to tell how the sutler has robbed our people for many years," Joe said. He was shaking just a little and he hoped it didn't show. "We all know about that."

"That is your opinion," Lester Matthews said.

"We have all suffered," Joe went on. For some reason he felt better because Lester Matthews had cut in. It gave him some strength. "We have put up with the sutler Linton and his thievery because we had no other choice. Arrowhead is far away. There is no easy way to get there. Our people want a change."

"Who says that?" Lester Matthews demanded to know.

"I now have seventeen families who employ me to buy supplies for them in Arrowhead," Joe said.

Lester Matthews snorted and looked at his fellow councilmen. "Seventeen families. What does that prove? More than four thousand of our people live at San Pedro."

"I have a small jeep," Joe said. "If I had a truck I could have seventeen more families and more beyond that."

"That still proves nothing," Lester Matthews said.

"It proves that many of our people are not happy with the sutler Linton," Joe said in a quiet voice. He was glad Lester Matthews kept answering him back. It only reinforced his feeling and he knew his plan was a good one. "It also proves supplies can be bought outside the reservation and can be delivered here for less than what the sutler Linton makes our people pay. And that includes expenses for gasoline and payment to me for my time."

Lester Matthews nodded. There was a sneer on his lips. "Yes, you've made a good thing out of that, haven't you?"

At this point Willis Chambers asked, "Just what is it that you're asking of the Council, Joe?"

Lester Matthews laughed. "It's pretty clear what he's after. He wants the Council to buy him a truck so he can make his business bigger and make more money. I can tell you right now, Murdock, the answer is no."

Joe did not bother to remind Lester Matthews he had no right to speak for the Council that way even though he was chairman. "I am not asking the Council to buy me a new truck," he said in the same quiet voice. He was much surer of himself now. He was beginning to feel strong.

Lester Matthews picked up his gavel to bang it, as though that was all there was to say. Joe held up his hand. Lester Matthews did not bring down the gavel.

"I am asking the Council to build a new store," Joe said.

Lester Matthews frowned again. "Build Mr. Linton a new store? What would that do?"

"I don't mean build the sutler Linton a new store," Joe said. "I mean build a new store for our people."

Now that it was out Joe felt as though a weight had been lifted from his back.

The councilmen looked at each other as though they didn't quite understand what he was talking about. Sam Hopkins was just as confused as anyone else.

163

"A store for the people?" Sam Hopkins repeated.

"I mean build a store the Council would run," Joe said. It was coming out easier and easier and he believed in it wholly again. "I mean build a store for all of us, a store where no profit would be made, where the lowest prices would be charged. I mean build a store all our people would own."

There was silence, a long, total silence. The councilmen were stupefied. The first movement was made by Nahilzay. Nahilzay turned away from his vision and put his old, dark eyes on Joe.

The action brought Lester Matthews back to life. "That's crazy! Apaches never owned a store!"

Nahilzay never took his eyes off Joe.

Thirty

Bill Hunter was going over some Bureau paper work with the Agent when Linton burst into Lawton's office. Hunter was astonished. Nobody ever entered the Agent's office without first being announced by Lawton's secretary.

The Agent was visibly irritated by this violation of protocol and probably would have said something to the storekeeper, particularly since his Deputy had witnessed it, but before the Agent could get a word out the sutler exploded with what had happened at the Tribal Council.

Lawton leaned back in his big chair, his riding crop held at both ends by his clenched hands. He listened in silence as Linton related what Joe had proposed to the Council. As Linton went on in a shrill, furious voice, a red flush started on the Agent's neck. It crept up onto his cheeks and made the little military moustache look like a tiny patch of snow.

Linton was hopping up and down now, and with his scraggly neck and messy head of hair he reminded Hunter of a mad wet hen.

"They listened to him!" Linton shouted, hitting the Agent's desk with his hand. "They listened to him!"

The Agent bent the riding crop slightly. His knuckles were as white as his moustache.

"And what did they decide?" Lawton asked calmly.

Hunter had to admire his control. He could mark the measure of his boss' rage but the voice was like a piece of ice.

"Matthews said the Council would consider the idea!" Linton screeched. "Consider the idea!"

"There was nothing else he could say," Lawton said. "The

Council is required to consider any suggestion made by a member of the tribe."

"Consider the idea!" Linton screamed again, as though the Agent had not spoken.

Hunter was shocked at the way Linton spoke to the Agent. He had never heard anyone address Lawton that way. He had the feeling that the conversation would have been different if he were not there. He tried to think of some way to get away gracefully. Get away and ponder over Joe Murdock's unprecedented idea. He was still bowled over by that.

Lawton got up and started pacing back and forth. He paused for a moment. His face was bleak. Suddenly he brought his whip down hard on the edge of his desk.

"He's a radical," Lawton said. His voice was still frozen. "I knew that from the start. You take a savage out of his natural element and you expose him to the civilized world and what happens? He becomes a radical."

He seemed about to go on, but he caught himself, possibly because he remembered his Deputy was there.

"All right, Thaddeus," he said. "Thank you for keeping me informed."

The sutler was not about to be fobbed off that simply. "Never mind all that," he said at the top of his voice. "The question is, what are you going to do about this?"

The Agent looked quickly at Hunter. "It is within the Council's legal rights to take such a step," he said to Linton.

"The hell with their legal rights!" Linton shouted, slapping the desk again. "How are you going to stop this?"

"Bill Hunter and I will discuss the matter," the Agent said, still talking slowly and calmly. "Hunter has listened to everything you have said, just as I have, and we will go over it thoroughly."

Linton finally got the message. He twisted his head and looked at Hunter, as though he were seeing him for the first

166

time, which might have been the case. Linton was still in a blind rage but he was not altogether a fool. He huffed a little while longer and then he took himself out.

When he was gone Lawton sat down and sighed. "Poor old chap. He's so emotional."

Hunter remembered the moment when the Agent had whipped his desk with the riding crop.

Lawton shrugged and picked up the memorandum he and Hunter had been studying. "But it's understandable, I suppose. He's put his life into that little store. It must come as a dreadful disappointment to him to find that some of the Indians here are so ungrateful."

Thirty-one

The autumn air was thin and sharp and the wind brought down a song from the north. In the old days the Apaches called this time of year Earth-Is-Reddish-Brown. The summer was over and it was cold and they could see their breath again.

The Apaches of San Pedro came to the Council building from all parts of the reservation. For some it was a journey of more than half a day. When every seat in the chamber had been filled they collected outside. All of them had heard of the incredible request Sgt. Joe Murdock had made. None of them believed anything would come of it, but it was a historic challenge and had to be marked. More importantly it gave them all an excuse to get together and talk about other things. They talked in the chamber and they squatted on the ground and talked outside and there the talking drove away some of the cold. The papooses fell asleep early. They were not bothered by the heavy smoking inside the building and outside they were wrapped warmly against the wind.

It was a big night at San Pedro. It was the biggest night for many years. The Council was going to vote on Joe Murdock's proposal. Nobody doubted the decision. Everybody knew the laws of life by this time. They all understood who was against what Joe wanted. But Joe was a warrior and warriors always had the right to speak and to be heard and in a way this was the first chance the tribe had to pay a kind of homage to Joe.

The Agent was sitting inside the chamber in a small, compact enclave of white Bureau personnel. The Agent had never had his discussion with Hunter but that had not surprised the Deputy. He had understood clearly that he had wanted to shut Linton up before he talked too much, before he said something damaging.

And what could that be, Hunter had wondered since. What could the sutler say that would be more shocking than the manner in which he spoke to the Agent that afternoon? The answer gnawed in Hunter's mind. Were those rumors correct after all? Were Lawton and Linton secret partners, as people had been saying for years?

In any case, Hunter would never look upon his chief with the same eyes again. Linton's arrogance, his rudeness, was something Hunter would never forget. The sutler operated on the reservation more or less at the pleasure of the Agent. Lawton could have sent him packing in five seconds. But he had not. He had listened to the sutler's abuse and had done nothing about it.

What the Agent had done was to notify the Council that he had become aware of Joe Murdock's proposal and that while he had a policy of not interfering in the internal affairs of the tribe he was responsible for the welfare of the people. On that basis he requested of the Council, if it were going to consider the proposal seriously, permission to address the body.

Lester Matthews gave a lot of thought as to whether it was necessary to consider Joe Murdock's suggestion, seriously or any other way. His first decision was just to forget it. But he put his politician's ear to the ground and changed his mind. The business just could not be ignored. Word had got round everywhere. People were talking about it. It had to be resolved in open meeting.

A section of the chamber had been reserved for the whites. The Agent had ordered members of the Bureau to attend. He wanted the full majesty of officialdom to be present as the Council debated the matter.

Bill Hunter looked around the room. The people showed

169

no emotion. He understood. It was the mask the Indians could put on their faces. He wondered, as he had before, how those faces were before the Apaches had had to wall them in against the white man.

He nodded to Jennie Gates. She wasn't quite able to hide her worry. Beside her were Oliver and Florence Murdock and they looked concerned too. Their son must be a worry to them, Hunter thought. It was funny in a way. There were so many white boys who were returning from this war with what their parents considered to be radical ideas. White parents from one end of the country to the other were experiencing the same fears, worries and confusion that the Murdocks had to contend with here in this Tribal Council.

A noteworthy absentee that evening was Thaddeus Linton. Hunter guessed he was elsewhere by order of the Agent. Linton was disliked by most of the Apaches and more than that he was too unstable to be left around loose.

Lester Matthews banged his gavel and opened the hearing. He explained why the meeting had been called. With great skill he managed to convey in his flat, professional voice that he believed the whole idea insane, but that as a fair-minded man, chairman of a fair-minded Council, he was bound to air the proposal.

"Mr. Townsend Lawton, our experienced Agent, has interested himself in this matter," Matthews said. "He has asked the Council's permission to speak on it. The Council is grateful for Mr. Lawton's continuing interest in the welfare of our people. The Council is honored to listen to him."

Lawton stood up and faced the twelve men. Nahilzay, on his separate side, gazed at the blank wall where his vision rested as though it were a picture on a screen, a picture only he could see. Or maybe the vision was on the other side of the wall and the wall was no wall at all but an opening to the beyond.

170

"Gentlemen," Lawton said to the councilmen. "I am here because you are wards of the government and it is my duty to protect you. You are under the protection of the government and I am the chief representative here of that government. But this is more than a duty for me. It is my deep, personal desire to watch over you and to give you advice when I see that you might because of lack of information and experience be at the point of making a bad mistake."

The chamber was very quiet. This was a ceremony. There weren't many ceremonies. The doors were open for fresh air and so that people outside might listen and pass the words along to the others who could not get close to the doors.

"I will not go into the time and effort that Mr. Linton has spent on your behalf all these long years," Lawton went on. "He has devoted his life and his energies to all of you, from a time before some of you were born. He set for himself the mission to bring to you the benefits of things available on the outside."

Joe Murdock sat rigid. His eyes were as fixed as Nahilzay's. He did not by a flicker react to any of the words the Agent spoke.

"But that is not the issue here," Lawton said. "Mr. Linton is not the issue at all. The issue is whether you all would be better served if you, as a tribe, owned and operated your own general store on the reservation. You have every right to do so, make no mistake about that. It is not within my power to deny this. The Charter gives you that privilege. And if I believed it would benefit the people of San Pedro I would be the first to encourage such a move."

Lawton paused and looked away from the Council to the people. His voice was quiet and reasonable.

"But I, as your agent, must tell you that in my considered opinion, such a step would be a disaster for the tribe. I will

171

tell you why I believe this. The management of a large store calls for many experiences and skills. You do not have those experiences and those skills. Managing a store is more than just standing behind a counter and taking orders from customers. Goods must be brought in from distant places. Contracts must be made. Accounts must be kept. Certain taxes must be paid. There are many complicated federal and state and county laws and regulations that must be obeyed. An endless stream of problems, gentlemen, and none of them part of your experience."

Lawton paused to let his words sink in.

Joe Murdock, unmoved, could see that some of the listeners, among the councilmen and in the audience, were nodding in agreement. And he had to concede the Agent was making a good case.

Perhaps he had been foolish about this. Perhaps it was not his place to take lonely stands. Things were as they were. It was hard to change things anywhere, even on the outside. The different establishments always seemed to hang together, even when they represented different people. As he listened to Lawton's smooth words and convincing way, he felt a deep, tired sadness.

"I speak to you from the heart," Lawton was saying now. "I speak as your friend and protector. It would take a good deal of money to construct and then equip and supply a store. I believe with all my heart you would be making a catastrophic mistake to gamble with that much money from your Tribal Fund. You have worked for years to put that money together. How sad it would be to see it go down the drain on a crazy venture. So, gentlemen, people of the tribe, as your Agent, as the representative of your government, I must take the official position of opposing this wild scheme. I must urge that you continue along the course that has proved safe and workable and beneficial in the past."

172

Lawton sat down. There was no applause because the Apaches could never understand the meaning of clapping hands together. But Joe could see, he could smell, that there were many people who agreed with every word the Agent had said. And there was something else. Linton, good or bad, was tradition.

The councilmen now talked among themselves, one man leaning over and speaking quietly into the ear of another. Then Lester Matthews rapped the gavel again and announced he would speak.

"The Agent has plainly spoken in our best interests," he said. "He has spoken with wisdom and affection."

Perhaps Lester Matthews would have said more but Sam Hopkins spoke up. He demonstrated his unfamiliarity with parliamentary rules. He did not ask permission. He just spoke.

"I favor Joe Murdock's proposal," Sam Hopkins said.

Lester Matthews fixed an unpleasant eye on him. He didn't like what Sam Hopkins had said, of course, but even more, he disliked the newcomer's disregard of the rules.

"You were his partner, weren't you?" Lester Matthews inquired.

"Yes," Sam Hopkins said.

"You still are, aren't you?"

"Yes," Sam Hopkins said.

Lester Matthews turned away. Everybody, including Sam Hopkins, who had never spoken in public before, knew that Sam had been put down. Sam Hopkins was too embarrassed to say anything more.

"Is there any other member of our Council who wants to speak before we put the matter to a vote?" Lester Matthews asked, looking this way and that.

There was no reply.

"If no one wants to speak we will take the vote," Lester Matthews said.

He raised his gavel but before he could bring it down, Joe stood up. There was a stir in the room.

"I want to speak," Joe said.

"You have already spoken to the Council," Lester Matthews said.

"I will speak again," Joe said.

There was more stirring around in the chamber and word was passed outside quickly. Many of the people in the room craned their necks and other people pressed into the open doorways. Some of them had never had a good look at Joe Murdock.

Lester Matthews made the quick decision not to have Joe quote the rules and regulations of the Charter again. "You may speak," he said. "Be brief."

The people settled back. They did not believe Joe would be brief. That was not the tradition. The tradition called for long talks and long listenings.

Joe faced the Council. He told himself he must keep his voice firm. "The Agent said we know nothing about running a store. The Agent is right."

Lawton wrinkled his forehead. The people looked puzzled.

"We know nothing about running a store," Joe said. "It is true. It is true that a century ago we knew nothing about raising cattle. Chief Cochise taught us we must learn the way of the white man or perish. We learned to raise cattle. We knew nothing then about growing things from the earth. Chief Cochise said we must learn or die. We learned. We know nothing about running a store. We can learn."

Joe sat down. His heart was pounding. He felt the loneliness again and he was a little scared. He had managed to keep his voice firm but these were important people, from the Agent on down, and he had spoken against them and in public.

The listeners in the audience, who had not considered Joe had even warmed up, were caught short. Even Lester Mat-

174

thews was surprised, although he had ordered Joe to be brief. He looked at Joe, half expecting him to stand up and say more. Then he crashed down the gavel.

"If there is nothing more to be said, we will vote," Lester Matthews said.

Joe raised his head sharply and then lowered it. He was beaten, he knew. He had never really expected to win, but now he knew for sure he was beaten.

He knew the Council always voted in secret and that ordinarily Lester Matthews now would have ordered the chamber cleared. But now Joe realized that Lester Matthews and the Agent had worked things out. Now each councilman would have to cast his vote under the cold eye of the Agent, in front of the rest of the Bureau.

Joe thought that some of the councilmen might object to this invasion of privacy. He looked at each face. No one did. Joe felt the loneliness again. He felt isolated in the room.

The voting started. Lester Matthews, as chairman, cast the first vote, resoundingly, against the proposition. A second councilman, another old hand, voted the same way. Then all three of the newly elected councilmen, led by Sam Hopkins, voted in favor of the Murdock proposition.

Joe sat up a little straighter in his seat. He knew he was defeated but it would not be a rout. He lowered his head. He was going down but in honor and he needed all his control. He did not want anybody to see his face.

Willis Chambers voted next. In a clear voice he said he favored the proposition.

Joe looked up sharply. He felt something crowding in his throat. It choked him.

Another councilman voted against the measure and three others followed quickly with no votes. That left it six to four, against. And then, to Joe's final amazement, the last two councilmen voted yes.

That left it six to six. Lester Matthews smiled. A brief expression of satisfaction passed across the Agent's face. The establishment had won. Linton had won. Nothing would be changed. A tie vote defeated a motion.

Joe breathed deeply. He had lost as he had known he would lose but he had not lost his dignity. What he had urged upon the Council had been considered seriously and half of the members had agreed with him.

He looked at the two men who had cast the two final votes in his favor. They were old-timers and they had known that all they could do was make the futile tie. They knew they would antagonize the Agent. They had done so. That was worth something.

Lawton, now concealing his pleasure, got to his feet, either to say something or to leave, although Lester Matthews had not yet officially declared the motion defeated.

Lester Matthews quickly banged his gavel. "The vote is even, six to six," he said. "I therefore declare, according to the rules of the Charter . . ."

There was a loud thump in the room. Lester Matthews stopped dead.

One thump and then a second. Everyone in the room turned to the sound.

Nahilzay, still staring across the years through the chamber wall, struck his war staff a third time on the wooden floor.

He said, "The young warrior speaks true."

Thirty-two

All of that took place almost three years ago. Since then there have been changes at the San Pedro Reservation.

First of all there is the Apache Supermarket. Perhaps it isn't the size supermarket you might find in a big shopping center on the outside, but the people at San Pedro look at it as the real thing. It's no more than maybe twice the size of Linton's old place but it seems much bigger because it's bright and airy and clean.

The food is on shelves and in bins and freezer compartments just like any self-service market anywhere. All day long Apache women with papooses on their backs push around little carts helping themselves to whatever they think they need.

They line up at the checking counter and take what they selected out of the carts and the checker runs the items up on the cash register and then the women sign the sales slip. Women who can't write scratch out an "X" and the checker puts down the woman's name.

The prices in the Apache Supermarket are good by current standards. They're a little lower than the prices in Arrowhead. They're about half, or less than half, of what Linton used to charge.

At the end of the first year of operation, after the cattle payoff, every account in the store was settled in full. Out of thousands of dollars of business there was found to be a discrepancy on the books of exactly $16.36. That was later traced to a bookkeeping error.

Joe Murdock manages the store. He couldn't sleep until he ran the deficit down.

There is a story about how Joe became manager. The Apaches talk about it among themselves still. It's become part of folklore and will be told from one generation to another.

After Nahilzay used his privilege as a life-member of the Council to cast the tie-breaking vote—the first time he had bothered to exercise that right in more than a quarter of a century—Lester Matthews banged his gavel again and this time he had to declare that the project was approved.

There was no reaction in the room. The people watched the Agent leave. The Agent showed nothing. One by one the other Bureau people left. Soon there were only Apaches in the chamber. Still no one gave any sign.

Once the decision was made, the Council showed it was smarter than the Agent might have believed. Acting as a solid unit, the first thing the Council did was send Joe Murdock to Phoenix to find out how to get things started.

Joe went to the Phoenix headquarters of one of the biggest chains of supermarkets in the West. He was shunted from one straw boss to another but he persisted and he finally worked himself into the office of the head man, Ted Crane, and as time went on the people at San Pedro got to know a lot about Mr. Ted Crane.

Crane sat behind his desk and he listened to Joe explain what the Apaches were planning to do. Joe was feeling that nervous thing again, the feeling of being alone at the end of a limb, there in that big office with that important businessman listening to him without saying anything. When Joe finished Crane called in his chief assistant and asked Joe to tell it all over again.

After all that he told Joe the first thing he needed was some education in the business of selling food. He told Joe the supermarket chain ran a school in Los Angeles to train store managers and he pulled some wires and got Joe enrolled. Then Crane took a trip to the San Pedro Reservation to look things over for himself.

Lawton washed his hands of the matter and turned it over to Bill Hunter. When Hunter met Crane for the first time he thought his name fit him better than any he had ever heard before. Ted Crane was a tall, skinny man with a long neck and a big Adam's apple. He loped around like a large bird.

Crane talked at length with Hunter and then with the councilmen. He made notes assessing Apache customs and likes and dislikes and then he went back to Phoenix. A few weeks later he returned to the reservation with an architect who worked for the chain. The architect studied everything and consulted with the Council and then drew up plans for the new store. Ted Crane gave these plans to the Apaches for free.

They started building while Joe was still in school in Los Angeles. The architect and a white contractor were put in charge of the project by the Council. Apache men helped build the structure. By the time Joe finished his training the store was standing.

Joe got high marks. Crane told that to everybody. Joe never mentioned it. Crane said Joe had absorbed just about everything they could teach him. Crane said that from Joe's school record he'd offer him a job anytime.

As Crane talked here and there he kept nodding his head about everything. He never seemed to get over what was going on. One of the things that threw him was the way the Council paid cash for everything out of the Tribal Fund. Cash on the line when bricks and cement and wood and glass were delivered. Cash on the line when services were performed.

As soon as the store was finished the trucks started rolling in from Phoenix with crates and cartons of merchandise. Some member of the Council was always waiting, ready with cash. Most of the truck drivers had never been paid cash before. They got used to it.

The building of the market and then the delivery of the goods became the greatest attraction for the San Pedro Apaches. They came from all sections of the reservation to watch. Some of the older people couldn't believe what they saw. Joe told them they owned it all, the store and the goods. They couldn't believe it. Some of them can't believe it yet.

Whether or not they believed that it belonged to them they were proud of what was going on. The Apache men would not allow the truckers to cart the supplies into the building. They insisted on doing that themselves to make sure nothing would be damaged.

As soon as the men brought in the cartons and opened them, the women set the cans on the shelves. They were even fussier than the men. They didn't like to see dents in cans. They turned a dented can around so the dent didn't show.

After that they cleaned out the place. The store was immaculate from the start. It still is. The women take care of the store the way they take care of their homes.

While the goods were arriving and being put into place Joe Murdock was a very busy man. He and Crane worked out the layout and at the same time Joe selected and instructed half a dozen young Apache men and women to work in the store. One of the youths was Henry Sloane.

Crane sat down with the Tribal Council and figured out a price structure. His goal was to keep prices as low as possible and at the same time give the Council a fair return on the investment from the Tribal Fund.

The day arrived finally for the formal opening. There were flags and pennants. There was a three-piece combo of Apache kids with guitars.

There was a newspaperman and a photographer from Phoenix and one of the radio stations there sent a man out to make a tape of the ceremony.

180

The store was opened by cutting a ribbon. Lester Matthews did the honors. He made a speech. Lester Matthews managed somehow to convey the impression he was responsible for everything. The Agent spoke briefly. He wished the people success. He did it gracefully. Joe tipped his hat to Lawton's style.

The Apaches listened to the Agent with respect. They appreciated the awkwardness of his position. Joe was proud of them. He was proud of his blood. Even in that time of their triumph the Apaches would not let the Agent lose face.

It was Joe Murdock who was their hero. He had to make a speech too. It was the shortest speech of all, which was a blessing in that Arizona sun. He thanked Ted Crane, who sat there bobbing his head as though he still couldn't believe what was happening.

Oliver and Florence Murdock were present and they couldn't believe it either. They couldn't believe their son had done all this and they didn't know whether it was altogether right and how it would end. They knew what the people thought of Joe though. They could see that and hear it. Oliver held his face tight. Florence Murdock thought her heart would burst.

Jennie Gates was there, of course. She didn't try to hide her feelings. While Joe was up there speaking she looked at him as though he was a god.

After the ribbon was cut the people poured in to have a look. Business wasn't scheduled to start until the next day. This was the time for wandering about.

That night there was a big party with the usual social dancing. Ted Crane was the star there. The Apache women, most of whom scarcely reached his chest, thought he was like someone from another world. They had never seen an Adam's apple like that. They fought to dance with him. Crane accommodated all of them. He was a great success.

The next day the Apache Supermarket opened for busi-

181

ness. That was the day Thaddeus Linton closed down. Joe showed right away he hadn't gone to that school for nothing. He made a deal with Linton to buy the store and all the unsold goods in it. He got everything at the price he offered, a fair price. Linton tried to hold him up but Joe stuck to his guns. He could have knocked the price down, he knew. Linton didn't have much choice.

Joe found himself feeling sorry for the sutler. Despite everything, he felt sorry. Linton looked old and shrunk down and more wrinkled and scrawny than ever. Joe couldn't help feeling sorry.

Linton's store still stands at San Pedro. Joe uses it for a warehouse. At first he thought about tearing it down to rid the reservation of the memory of Linton but then he thought it would be better to let it stand. It was a reminder of many things. It was a reminder of a victory. It makes everybody feel strong when they look at it.

There are a few other changes on the reservation. Willis Chambers is chairman of the Council. Lester Matthews is still in office but he doesn't talk much and he doesn't swing much weight.

Maybe part of the reason for that is that Bill Hunter is Agent now.

Lawton retired about six months after the store opened. Times had changed too much for him, he said. Hunter was surprised to learn that the Bureau in Washington had promoted him to take Lawton's place. He hadn't expected that. He figured there were too many bad marks put down on his record by Lawton.

Joe Murdock and Jennie are married. They have a little papoose and another one is on the way. They have dinner now and again with the Hunters and Bill and Winnie go to their house. When Joe and Jennie want a night in town or a weekend in Phoenix they bring the baby over to the Hunters.

Unless Oliver and Florence Murdock make a fuss. The Murdocks have finally got to be pretty proud of Joe and what he did. But the Hunters manage to get to keep the baby often enough. Their children have long since flown the nest and they like to hear a baby squalling again, especially a baby named Bill.

Every once in a while Bill Hunter and Joe get into Hunter's car and drive off the reservation. They drive to the profile of Cochise. They talk over their problems. They talk over many things.

ABOUT THE AUTHOR

Born and raised in New York City, Elliott Arnold attended New York University. In 1934 he went to work for the New York *World-Telegram* and in that same year, at the age of twenty-two, saw the publication of his first novel. Twice awarded the Commonwealth Club of California Medal for Fiction, for *Blood Brother* and *Flight from Ashiya*, Mr. Arnold is the author also of *A Night of Watching*, a novel of Nazi-occupied Denmark, which received wide critical acclaim, and most recently, *Forests of the Night*, a fast-moving story of modern Germany.

Mr. Arnold has written several books for younger readers, including *A Kind of Secret Weapon* in which he utilized to considerable advantage the same research into World War II that had earlier found its way among his adult material. American Indians, as the present book testifies, are another area of deep interest for him, one which concerns him in his daily life as well as his creative work.